"Is it possible to have too many vampire stories? SANGUINARY shows there is room for one more. Cops with stakes and vampires intent on ruling—only problem is that love is stronger than blood. A nicely written vampire cop romance."
—Robert E. Vardeman, author of *Fate of the Kinunir*

## THROUGH DARKEST TEMPTATION

When Dallas police detective Cami Davis joined the city's vampire unit, she planned to use the job as a stepping-stone to a better position in the department. She didn't know then what she knows now: A silent war rages between humans and their supposedly pacified predators, and the vampires are winning. With the clock running out on her kind, Cami will do whatever she must to defeat the "Sanguinary."

Enter Reese Fulton, a disaffected ex-cop and a vampire. She can't exactly trust him, but with his cowboy boots and good-ole-boy drawl he's the perfect beard for Cami's fledgling undercover operation. Yet playing Reese's Claimed—a vampire's personal bloodgiver— isn't as straightforward as she was led to believe. His bite is as enthralling as his dimpled smile, and soon Cami is wondering which will pose more of a challenge: subduing the enemies of humanity…or her own desire.

# SANGUINARY

## Margo Bond Collins

Night Shift Book 1

www.BOROUGHSPUBLISHINGGROUP.com

SANGUINARY

ISBN 978-1-942886-68-6

*This book is dedicated to my Miller clan—*
*because we all know a good story is better than the truth every time.*

# ACKNOWLEDGMENTS

First and always, thanks to all the readers out there—without you, this book would never have seen the light of day. Thanks to my family for love, care, and dinner on a regular basis. My eternal gratitude to the BICs, because I don't think I could write without you and the super-sexy word sprints. Thanks always to the Taylors for being my best friends for so long. As always, to Deb for keeping me connected to this world, even when my head is in the one I'm creating. To The Vampirarchy: You're the best street team an author could ask for. A few extra special thanks this time: to Pam, for adventures in moving. To Phil, for listening with love. To Clint, for reminding me to laugh. To Amber, for being so unbelievably kind and supportive. To Elyse, for always knowing what I should watch next. To Lateia, for WD plans. To Melanie, for figuring all this out first. You all make my life a better place to live, and I love you all. Huge thanks to my editor, Camille, for catching the story problems, appreciating grammar trivia, and debating the subjunctive. I love working with you! Special thanks to the cover artist for making *Sanguinary* (and Reese!) look so hot! And to everyone at Boroughs: You're amazing. Any mistakes are my own—and anyone I missed, know that I appreciate you all more than words could ever say.

# Table of Contents

# SANGUINARY

# Prologue

"You were first on the scene, right? Tell me what we've got," I said to the uniformed officer—a T. Vargas, her badge told me—standing white-faced on the edge of a ring of yellow and black crime-scene tape. She swallowed convulsively, her gaze flicking toward the body splayed on the flagstones a few feet away.

Red and blue lights strobed across the front of the Winspear Opera House. Squad cars had pulled up onto the sidewalk, blocking any foot traffic past the outdoor parking-lot elevators and through the main artery into the theater. Not that pedestrians were likely at three in the morning in the arts district—presumably the reason for the body's placement near the elevators on the broad expanse of flagstones between the building and Flora Street in Dallas.

At least there was only one body this time.

"We were on patrol." Vargas gestured toward her partner, currently talking to the manager of the opera house several yards away. "We'd driven by here maybe two hours earlier and hadn't seen anything. I don't know if the body was here already, but we didn't see it then. This time, I saw the dress from the street."

I paused, taking a moment to survey the scene, my notebook still tucked away in my front jacket pocket. The dead woman's dress was a deep red, matching the Winspear's interior decor, visible through the darkened glass of the walls curving away from us.

I pulled the notebook out of my pocket and plucked a pen from its place in the bun I habitually wore at crime scenes. "Okay," I said, pen poised to take notes. "So you stopped?"

"Yes. I checked for a pulse, and then called for a bus and backup." Her voice shook. "And there was"—her finger spun in a circle, pointing overhead—"a weird, blue light coming from the victim's wounds, shooting straight up into the sky."

I glanced back at the body, at the strange symbols carved into the pale skin. "How long did the light last?"

Vargas shrugged. "It was gone by the time the ambulance arrived."

Vargas was clearly a rookie, not expecting anything like this on her beat—especially since the other recent body dumps had been in residential neighborhoods. She was uncertain what to do with information that didn't easily fit into any police-academy crime-scene course manual. Having seen the odd blue lights at another scene, I knew exactly how eerie they were.

"Anything else?" I tried to keep my voice professional, no matter how gentle I wanted to be with her. Kindness from a female detective was almost always construed as weakness—even more so with me, given my small frame.

Vargas shook her head. "Johnson secured the scene while I stayed with the victim."

*Weird blue lights be damned. Good for her.*

I nodded. "Thanks, officer. Be sure to be detailed in your report, okay?"

There wasn't much to go on—though the earlier patrolling pass perhaps gave us a timeline. The rookie fled toward the squad car she'd arrived in, clearly thankful to get away from the scene. I watched her go and shook my head, not sure that one would make it on the job.

Then again, she had stayed with the victim in spite of those strange lights, so she might do fine.

No trace remained of any otherworldly glow now. Taking a step closer to the body, I dropped down and sat back on my heels, leaning sideways a bit to peer more closely at a small flutter that caught my eye. I started to drop one knee to the flagstones, but the dark gray pantsuit I wore was new from Neiman Marcus and had been out of my price range, even on sale. I didn't want to risk tearing it. It wasn't the best choice for a crime scene, but I'd been out to dinner when I got the call—the second time I'd bailed on a date for this case.

*Doubt I'll hear from the guy again. Just as well, really.*

"Hey, Bradley." I beckoned the crime-scene tech, who had finally arrived and was snapping on gloves. "Is that a piece of paper under the vic's head?"

He bent down over my shoulder to get a clearer view from my line of sight. "It's tangled in her hair." He pulled a pair of long tweezers out of his kit and snagged the sliver. "Yep. There's a word written on it." We both peered at the brownish, spidery writing.

"*Sanguinary*," I said. "Is that written in blood?"

"Maybe. I'll get the lab to run a basic analysis on it. If it's blood, we'll be able to let you know pretty quick if it's human and, if so, what type. DNA will take longer."

I stared at the woman a little longer. Her dark hair—almost the same color as mine—spilled out around her, matted with dark, coagulating blood. The two bloody marks on her neck shone like black stars on a white background.

*Vampire.*

I knew that if I lifted her dress, there would be other puncture wounds all over her body, and strange symbols carved across her skin: pentagrams within circles and other ritualistic signs. Exactly like the others. Ten murders in the four weeks since the beginning of September—all centered in downtown Dallas, and many of affluent victims whose families demanded action.

The department had been in a barely suppressed uproar.

I stood up, my knees popping a little. Five years ago, they wouldn't have done that.

And five years before that? Vampires hadn't existed, except in books and B movies.

It took time for the world to believe. We hadn't even realized how to fight back when they'd first shown up.

This victim's ragged, bloody fingernails suggested she had tried to resist but obviously failed.

The red dress she wore would have originally matched the color of the relatively scant splashes of blood surrounding her, but those stains had dried to a muddy brown, the same color as the writing on the paper caught in her hair.

Her clothing suggested she'd been at the opera that evening, though the manager, roused from her bed, swore the building had been cleared and empty when she left.

One black, high-heeled pump lay several feet away, toppled over onto its side, the heel broken, as if she had stumbled out of the shoe when it failed her as she ran from a pursuer.

*Sanguinary.*

This was the third time the word had shown up in the case. The first time it had been left on a victim's voicemail by a man calling from an untraceable burner phone: "The Sanguinary expects you at the blood house tomorrow night."

The second time, it had been part of a to-do list in a victim's day planner: *Meet with vampire admin. + Sanguinary.*

I'd heard the word even before that from vampires I had taken down—whispered as a threat, shouted as a warning: *The Sanguinary is coming. The Sanguinary will kill you all.*

But no one who knew what the Sanguinary was would admit to it.

That's why I was about to go undercover among the vampires.

# Chapter 1

A week later, my partner, Quentin Garrett, and I didn't speak as we left the unmarked car, heading to meet my new vampire contact. Garrett's hands were twitching, as if he couldn't decide what to do with them. We parked on Commerce Street and crossed the road, heading east toward the local underground blood house, a semi-secret haven for local vampires and their hangers-on.

At the corner, Garrett stopped and looked me over. I wore a thin, dark green sweater over black pants.

"Here," he said, tugging at my sweater until it stretched to expose my right shoulder and the ropy remains of an old wound from a vampire arrest gone bad. "It's considered a come-on to show off your scars."

I shivered, and not from the cold. With one hand, I checked the placement of my wireless earpiece.

"You hear us, Iverson?" I asked quietly.

"Loud and clear." The lieutenant's tinny voice echoed in my head. "You need us, say the word—we're right around the corner."

Tonight was only the insert, I reminded myself, the set-up for what we all hoped would become deep cover, a chance to gain access to the upper echelons of the secretive Vampire Administration.

Iverson had played his part a few weeks before by firing me for supposedly screwing up case after case. Pretty much every case I'd touched since I had agreed to go undercover had turned to shit, all by design.

The vamps weren't supposed to know who I really was, but we were playing it safe, creating a cover story to use if the vamps traced me back to the department.

The case screw-ups might have been faked, but I'd been surprised by how real the red in my cheeks had burned as I'd packed a box and left the precinct. Even if many of my coworkers knew what was going on, it was humiliating.

The whole thing—my "firing," the move to get me connected to the local vamp clan, all of it—was a rush job, but for all we knew, we might have been playing to an empty house. The Dallas PD didn't necessarily have the Vampire Admin's full attention.

In fact, vampires weren't terribly interested in human laws, as far as we could tell, for all that we kept trying to legislate the vamps out of existence. In most states, including Texas, it was technically illegal to be a vampire, feed a vampire, or even associate with a vampire. It had been for almost six years now. New York had passed the first anti-vamp laws, not long after some vigilante group up there had caught a vampire alive—or undead, anyway—and handed it over to a government group to be analyzed. I always imagined that vampire being slowly carved up and dissected, never quite dying.

Anyway, it didn't take long for vampires to be labeled a threat on all levels: national, state, and local (though much of California was still holding out as various "vampire protection" groups tried to have the vamps classified as either people or an endangered species). Three different levels of anti-vampire task forces led to the usual kinds of interdepartmental squabbles, but it meant there was always someone to call in if you had a vampire problem.

And having the laws on the books allowed us to create the Paranormal Victims Units, also known as the Sucker Squads, ostensibly to take down any vampires we ran across. But everyone knew that the Vampire Administration didn't allow the squads anywhere near the important vamps.

When it came right down to it, the laws were a convenient fiction, designed to make us feel better about the monsters that had invaded our world. The official policy wasn't quite stake on sight, but it wasn't that far off. Vamps didn't have to do much to get offed, though everyone on the squads knew that if we pushed too hard, the vamps would push back.

But we kept trying.

As Garrett and I headed down the street toward the blood house, my partner pushed his shirtsleeves up until the vampire bite marks on his inner elbows showed clearly, like ammo loaded into a bandolier, marching up his arm and tracing along the blue vein that showed underneath. There were more of them since the last time I'd looked.

Even with all the time Garrett had spent in the blood house, he hadn't been able to learn anything about the Sanguinary.

Of course, I didn't know how hard he'd tried, really.

I wasn't sure how fucked up Garrett really was—or rather, whether or not it mattered that Garrett stayed seriously fucked up, both physically and mentally. Knowing he wasn't a hundred percent made me more wary than I might have been otherwise.

"You good?" he asked, glancing at me out of the corner of his eye. I wanted to make him stop and go over the plan one more time, but really, it was fairly straightforward.

"Good enough," I replied. "We get in; I pretend to hook up with some cowboy vampire; we get out."

Garrett stopped, staring at me intently, forcing me to halt too. "It's not that simple," he said. "You're setting up to go undercover for what might be a long time. Reese Fulton is the only vampire contact I have who even admits to knowing about the Sanguinary. You can't get into vampire high society without him, so we need you two to get close. You've got to act like you want this."

"I know, I know." I turned my back on my partner and headed up the street. "I'll shake the jitters before we get there."

Someone has to get in, I told myself, and Garrett wasn't in good enough shape to handle long-term deep cover—that much was obvious, even if no one in the brass wanted to talk about his recent relapse. But we all knew he'd been spending too much time with vamps. It's what bite addicts did.

We rounded the corner and walked two blocks. Garrett stopped in front of a plain, redbrick building in the middle of the third block and rang a buzzer. There was a pause, and someone buzzed us into the building. I couldn't decide which thought bothered me more—that they had some sort of camera and recognized Garrett, or that they might let anyone in.

The outside of the building might have been nondescript; the inside was anything but. The door opened into a beautifully decorated foyer. A tall, thin man in a tuxedo took our coats and hung them in a small closet off to the left, then motioned us through an arched doorway behind him.

In the main room, I glanced around to get my bearings. An enormous crystal chandelier hung down from the ceiling, casting a sharp, glittering light across the scene below. The balcony overlooked the central area, a marble-tiled room with white floors and burgundy velvet drapes covering the walls and windows. A black marble staircase curved up to the balcony on each side of the room.

At the very back, a bartender manned a bar made of dark wood. As I watched, several people (or maybe vampires) slipped through the door that stood directly behind the bar, always sure to close the heavy wood behind them.

Dark niches lined the walls under the balcony, many with velvet drapes drawn across them. The ones that were open held couches, some of them with figures draped across them—sleeping or dead, I wasn't sure. People—humans? vampires? both?—stood in small groups on the balcony and on the ground floor. Soft, baroque chamber music swayed through the room from a hidden sound system, notes from the flutes dancing across the deeper sound of stringed instruments.

And it smelled like blood. The coppery tang of it shivered on the back of my tongue.

"What do we do now?" I whispered to Garrett.

"Let me deal with it," he whispered back, scanning the room. Then he lifted his hand in greeting to someone I didn't see and headed across the room.

I took a deep breath and followed him.

We passed several small groups of people, many of whom turned to watch as we walked by. I heard several hisses—the sort that vampires make—as we passed. We were walking through a room full of vampires. And their willing victims.

The blood houses were an open secret—technically illegal, but ignored by both sides of the fight, as they gave a place for vamps to feed with minimal violence. It wasn't a perfect solution, but giving the vampires access to a ready food supply helped keep the fragile peace. Doesn't mean I actually wanted to see a blood house up close and personal. I didn't, and I hadn't.

My partner, though, seemed to know his way around this one.

Garrett weaved through the crowd until he came to two women standing together by the bar.

One of the women, a tiny brunette with a pageboy haircut and bright pink lipstick, sidled up to him, sliding across the two feet separating them with eerie vampiric grace. She wore a strapless pink dress, satin on the bodice, taffeta puffing out in a tea-length cloud around her. Her makeup was heavy over her pale skin, her bright blue eyes lined in a matching shade.

"Garrett, you're back." Her voice was high, like a child's—totally different from any vampire I'd heard before. Most of them aimed for "sultry." This one seemed to be going for "cute."

"And you're still not Claimed." The other woman was the sultry one. Black dress, black hair, black eyeliner, black everything to highlight her white, white skin. Even her voice sounded dark.

"This is Cami." Garrett gestured toward me. "She's not Claimed either, but she might be looking."

*Claimed?*

"Are you looking, Garrett?" the small one asked.

"Maybe." He smiled at her, his voice playful. My stomach curdled at the intimacy I heard there—and at the realization that my partner hadn't fully briefed me on what to expect tonight.

"Your friend doesn't like it when you flirt," the taller one said.

I glared at her. Vampires should not know more about me than I do.

"I'll have to see that she gets over it," a voice drawled from behind me. I whipped my head around in time to see a man standing up from a barstool behind me. I hadn't even noticed he was there.

God knows how I could have missed him.

He wore jeans and a dark blue, button-down shirt. He had on dark brown cowboy boots, and as he turned away from the bar, he picked up a black felt cowboy hat from the seat next to him, placing it on his head. On anyone else, I might have assumed that the hats and boots were an affectation. On him, they looked perfect. He was utterly beautiful, with bright green eyes and dark hair that curled down to barely brush the back of his collar.

*I am undercover,* I reminded myself sternly. *Here to do a job.*

When Garrett caught my gaze in his, flicking his glance toward the cowboy vamp, it was all I could do to keep from sighing aloud.

Would it have killed my partner to be a little more descriptive when he briefed me?

Of course that was the vampire cowboy I had to get close to tonight.

*No making eyes at the informants, Cami.*

But damn, he was hot.

"Nice scars." His gaze skimmed along my bared shoulder.

"Thanks," I said, almost breathless.

*And I am absolutely not attracted to vampires.*

I could keep telling myself that.

"But I thought you didn't do un-Claimed strays, Reese." The short woman managed to both pout and smile at the same time.

"I might make an exception for this one, Dahlia," he said.

"Really?" the taller woman asked. She eyed me critically. "I don't see anything especially interesting there."

"Then you aren't paying close enough attention," Reese said, his voice sliding across my spine like velvet. I shivered, forcing myself not to try to shake it off.

"Apparently." Her nostrils flared. She sniffed the air ostentatiously, and I got the impression that she intended to snub me. But then her expression changed. She tilted her head and looked at Garrett, then drew closer to me, closing her eyes and drawing deep breaths.

"Who is this?" she asked Reese.

He smiled at her. "Not for you."

With a sneer, she flipped her hair and turned her back on us, stalking away.

"Would you like to join me in one of the private rooms?" Reese asked me.

*Yes.* My stomach clenched at how quickly the thought formed.

*I am in so much trouble.*

"Sure." I hoped the vamps couldn't hear the way my heart raced. "It's why we're here."

"Oh, goody," said Dahlia, still not looking at me. "Does that mean you'll come away with us, Garrett?"

He shifted his eyes toward me. "I don't know, Dahlia. It's been a while."

I leaned forward and rested my fingertips on Garrett's arm, hoping to remind him that he'd promised not to get a fix while he was here. But I couldn't say anything—not without blowing my cover.

Reese's hands reached out to encircle my waist, and he pulled me back against his chest. "Leave it alone," he breathed into my ear, so quietly that I felt the words more than heard them.

I forced myself to stay still, ignoring the vampire's presence at my back, his hands on my body.

This was the first time I'd let one get this close since the arrest-gone-wrong that had left me with the scars.

And definitely the first time I'd ever thought of wanting to let him get even closer.

Crap. Big trouble. Vampires usually horrified me, with their cold, cold skin and their predatory eyes. But this one didn't repel me, and I worried about what that meant.

My reaction could mean that I was reading an interest in saving humanity, not devouring it—that was, according to Garrett, part of why Reese was an informant.

Or maybe it meant he was a better actor than most of them.

Garrett's gaze flickered back and forth between me and Dahlia.

"Goodness," said Dahlia. "Your friend is worried about you? But, sweetie," she turned to me, "I'll take care of him. Garrett never gets hurt when I take care of him." She placed a proprietary hand on his arm.

I stared steadily at Garrett.

*I have to maintain my cover.* I repeated it over and over to myself, a mantra that did little to convince me I was doing the right thing by letting Garrett go with the vampire women.

"Have fun," I finally managed.

"Come with me." Reese's hand moved down my arm, his fingers entwining in mine, and he moved away from Garrett and Dahlia, pulling me along behind him. I watched Garrett over my shoulder as I went. Not until Reese snapped a velvet curtain shut did I realize that he had led me into one of the alcoves under the balconies.

I meant to ask him what the sniffing business with Dahlia's companion had been about, but I forgot everything else when he pushed me down onto the red velvet couch that took up most of the space in the alcove.

"I told Garrett it was a bad idea to meet in a blood house," he hissed at me. For the first time since he'd spoken up at the bar, he actually sounded like a vampire. The irises of his eyes were beginning to glow the blue of a vampire's bloodlust—a color I had learned to loathe during my time on the Sucker Squad.

"So why didn't we meet elsewhere?" I asked. "And what's a stray?"

He ignored my first question. I knew the answer, anyway—we had met here because a vampire meeting a human anywhere else might draw suspicion from both sides of an undeclared war.

"Anyone who hasn't been Claimed." He continued before I could ask, "Being Claimed creates a bond between a vampire and bloodgiver. A vampire can always tell where his Claimed bloodgivers are, sometimes what they're thinking or doing."

I shuddered at the thought of such an intimate connection with the monsters I hunted.

Reese leaned back a bit. "You don't know what Garrett did to get you in, do you? He told the administrator he had someone who wanted to be Claimed," he said, narrowing his eyes and tilting his head to one side.

I froze. "What?"

Reese's voice dropped. "Your partner had been banned from the blood houses. He really didn't tell you anything, did he?"

*Oh, shit.*

"Shh," Reese whispered, holding one hand up to forestall any comment from me. Suddenly, he was over me, his knee pressing down the cushion between my legs, his arms pinning me to the back of the couch, his body hovering inches above mine.

I stared into his face, breathless with some combination of anger and anxiety. The vampire's eyes flared an even brighter blue, the color creeping out to cover the natural green of the irises.

Over his shoulder, I saw the curtain twitch open. The taller of the two female vampires I'd seen earlier—the sniffer—poked her head into the room.

"You two want company?" she asked, flashing her fangs in a predatory smile.

"Go away, Katrina," Reese said.

"You want this one all to yourself, I see. Fine. Go ahead and be greedy. See if I care." But she didn't leave. She stepped inside and leaned against the frame of the wall that separated our alcove from the next one. "Can't I at least watch?" she cajoled. "I promise I won't touch."

"Get. Out." Reese was practically growling.

"Okay, okay." She heaved a big sigh. "But I'll be out in the main room if you change your mind."

She left, the curtain swaying shut as she dropped it back into place.

Reese leaned back but didn't move from his position over me. "You can't leave this room without being bled."

"Bled?" I was pretty sure I sounded and looked as horrified as I felt.

"Addicts like your partner aren't welcome here. But then he offered to bring someone new." Reese watched me carefully. "If you leave this room without being bled, it will put all of us in danger."

My breath caught in my throat, and I pressed my lips together, unwilling to respond.

Had Garrett really used me to get back into the blood house? Or was that just part of the undercover op?

"How will anyone know if I've been bitten tonight?" I realized I had been unconsciously running my fingertips over my scars when I saw Reese's gaze tracking the movement.

"They'll smell it." He leaned in close to me again, breathing in deeply. "You've been bled before," he whispered, running his own finger lightly over the scars on my shoulder.

I whimpered. I couldn't help myself. But then I pulled myself together enough to say, "Not voluntarily." My heart beat wildly against my ribcage, and I fought to maintain some air of professional detachment.

His hand trembled and he pulled it away from me.

"I won't hurt you." He leaned his face in and nuzzled my shoulder.

"Oh, God." I shuddered, my voice quavering as I lost all pretense of calm. "Please don't. I don't want to end up like Garrett. Please. This was supposed to be for show."

He drew back a little and looked into my eyes. The glowing blue had taken over his irises entirely and was spreading out to cover the whites of his eyes. The eerie glimmer matched the light that had shone from the victims at the crime scenes. I was certain the two were connected, though I couldn't do more at the moment than file the similarity away in my back-brain, to be examined later.

"You won't end up an addict, Cami," Reese whispered, his voice hoarse. "This is for show. But I have to take some. If I don't, those vampires out there will begin to suspect that you're not what you seem. And if that happens, they might not let either of us out of here alive."

"Are you sure? Maybe they'll ignore us." I knew I sounded desperate, but I didn't care.

He chuckled and his voice regained some of its normal timbre. "Sweetheart, I just took a woman into a bleeding room for the first time in…well, in a very long time. Longer than some of those people have even been vampires. Believe me, they're going to be paying attention to us when we walk out of here."

"A woman?" I said, a little wildly. "Does that mean that you've brought men here?"

"No," he whispered, leaning in again and putting the full weight of his body against mine. "Not men. Not women. No one."

"Promise you won't take too much?" My voice was small and breathy.

"Yes," he whispered against my neck.

"Okay." I hardly even voiced the word.

And then his fangs were in my shoulder, slicing cleanly through the knotty scar tissue, sliding into the muscle below.

I had tensed, prepared for pain, but the hurt didn't come—not like I expected, anyway. It was more like a needle sliding in: a sudden, sharp pinprick, then gone.

And then it was all pleasure.

"Oh," I gasped in surprise, then deeper, "oh."

Reese moaned as his mouth worked against my shoulder.

"Um. Cami?" Lieutenant Iverson's voice echoed in my ear.

Dammit. I had forgotten they were listening in.

Apparently, Reese heard it too, because he pulled away from me and sat up.

"I'm here, Iverson." My voice shook.

"Everything okay in there?"

"Fine," I said quietly. I had regained control of my voice, at least.

"Need us to come in?"

"No. I'll be out in a bit." I pulled my sweater up over my shoulder, as if Iverson could possibly see me, and pulled the plug on the wire. I'd reconnect it later. After I regained some composure.

I patted my dark, shoulder-length hair into place and glanced at Reese. His eyes had returned to their normal green.

"Is that good enough?" I asked.

He grinned at me wryly. "I guess it'll have to do, since you brought a chaperone."

I ignored that bit, plugging the wire back in. Reese pulled the curtain aside, ushering me back into the main room with his palm on the small of my back. I took a step out and was suddenly glad for his steadying hand; I felt dizzy and breathless for a moment. I didn't know if it was the events of the last twenty minutes or the effect of all the vampiric eyes on me.

Reese had been right: The vampires stared at us as we came out of the alcove. And did more than stare too. They drifted closer, eyeing me up and down. Several of them even slid up beside me and circled around us, their noses twitching in the air like predatory animals scenting their prey. I glanced at Reese a little anxiously. He didn't look back at me, though. He was too busy staring down the most aggressive of the sniffers. One woman even tried to touch me, but Reese snarled, lifting one side of his lip and revealing a fang. The female vamp backed off.

"I think that's enough for tonight." Reese glanced over his shoulder at the retreating vamp and steered me toward the exit.

"Mmm," I murmured in agreement. I had planned to have Reese introduce me around so I could start to get to know the other players in the Dallas vamp scene. But I didn't feel up to it now.

That was fine. Tonight was all about show—setting me up as Reese's blood-tramp, giving us a public reason to spend more time together later as he worked to gain entry into the Vampire Admin and learn more about the Sanguinary.

We had certainly accomplished our goal for the evening.

I tamped down a shudder.

Even I couldn't have said if it was a tremor of revulsion or desire.

# Chapter 2

Two days later, staring at the reports from the Winspear Opera House scene, as well as photos from a brand new, West End crime scene, I was fairly certain it was revulsion—even if the twinges coming from the fang-marks Reese had left in my shoulder suggested otherwise.

For the first time in the investigation, the crime-scene photographer had caught the eerie blue light that had appeared at every scene. In the picture, it swirled up from the new victim's body, the beams bending in to meet one another in a bright blue spark about five feet off the ground and reflecting off the back windows of the Dallas County Administration Building—better known by its former name, the Texas School Book Depository.

If this had been the first victim, I would have looked for some significance to the body's placement near Dealey Plaza. But this was victim number eleven, and there was no discernible pattern in where the killer was leaving the bodies.

I scanned the lab report from the opera house crime scene. According to the technician, the word *Sanguinary* had been written in human blood—B-negative, the same type as the victim's, though a DNA match wouldn't be available for a few more weeks. But the vic had the same kind of blood crusted on her right index finger and some residue of what might be the same kind of paper. The report was carefully worded to avoid making any definite claims, but I could read the lab tech's opinion through all the science-speak: The victim, now identified as Felicia Monroe, had almost certainly scrawled the word in her own blood, then hidden the paper in her hair. Or maybe the perp had used her finger and done it.

Moving to the reports on the victim, I read that Felicia Monroe hadn't gone to the opera that night. She was a buyer for a local department store. Her husband thought she was away at a professional convention in Shreveport, but she had never shown up at her destination, according to both the Shreveport Convention Center and the Hilton where she had reservations. No one had known she was missing, but she had been away from her family for at least four days before she showed up dead in the Arts District.

I turned my attention back to the photos from the new crime scene.

This time, the vic was a vamp-junkie, all thin hair and papery, yellowed skin. But like the others, her body had been stretched out, arms and legs pointing in four different directions, abdomen and thighs covered in strange, spiky symbols. She also had deep holes gouged into what few meaty parts she had left.

I was uncomfortably reminded of Garrett. I probably should have paid more attention to him, should have noticed his downward spiral. I'd even seen some of the wounds on his arms, running up the insides of his elbows like track marks. But he'd told me that they were old. He said that they healed more slowly because of his addiction, not uncommon for cops who had been deep undercover. He claimed that his doctor was working on it. And it never occurred to me to ask the squad doc to verify his story, because I assumed that Garrett would never lie to me.

We were partners—had been for three years, since I'd come up through the ranks and made detective, albeit on the Sucker Squad.

He had been my mentor since I had joined the specialized squad.

I had wanted to be a homicide detective, solving the mysteries of why: why murder, why him, why her, why kill at all?

And I guess I was in homicide. But the homicides we investigated all had the same solution: vampires.

I was the first woman on the Sucker Squad, but the distinction was short-lived. Jeanie Vincent had been promoted less than a month later. All things considered, I preferred having another female detective on the squad to any prestige I might have gained from being the only woman in the unit. And I liked Jeanie's no-nonsense approach to the job, especially compared to Garrett's desire to feed the monsters.

Even so, I had been absolutely certain that Garrett always had my back.

Until that night three months ago.

It had been Garrett's night off, so I took the lead when Jeanie and I answered a resident's call reporting vampire-related activity in her building. There was probably also drug-related activity, given the neighborhood, but the caller hadn't seemed concerned about that.

I was the first one into the dingy basement room. I kicked in the door and saw three vampires—two female, one male—all fastened like lampreys on a mostly naked human on the floor.

I didn't even recognize Garrett at first. His face was contorted into a grimace that was half pain and all pleasure. I was already partway across the room before my mind processed what my eyes were seeing and I stumbled to a halt, turning away from the sight.

"Get him out of here," I said to Jeanie, who had moved up behind me and placed a hand on my shoulder. I jerked away from her. "Not now. Deal with him."

She nodded and slid past me, pulling the vamps away from Garrett's prone body. I cringed at the sucking, ripping sound their mouths made as they were torn away from his skin. They snarled, but backed away from the long knife Jeanie brandished at them after she nicked the throat of the closest one. I backed her up with a stake, and the vamps huddled in the corner.

"No." Garrett moaned and stretched his arms toward the last vamp who'd been pulled away.

Suddenly, the room was too hot. I could smell the sweat, the blood. It smelled like sex and violence.

Bile rose in my throat and my stomach clenched. I stumbled blindly back up the stairs and outside, gulping the cool night air.

Jeanie led Garrett up the stairs. His eyes were glazed.

My teeth clenched. "Okay. Let's get out of here." I jerked my chin toward the unmarked car I was driving. Garrett's eyes focused in on me.

"Cami," he murmured.

I shook my head and got into the front seat while Jeanie directed the uniforms who had joined us to clear out the nest.

"Okay," she said after guiding Garrett into the back seat. "We're ready."

We kept the windows rolled down, but the rotten-meat stench of the vampire den kept wafting toward us from Garrett's clothing.

It hadn't occurred to me then to ask why he'd been in the basement rather than a blood house, where the blood-taking was at least formalized, and presumably controlled.

With a shudder, I shook off the memory. I had more important things to do now, like figure out who was killing women in Dallas, why they sucked the life out of their victims, and why they left pentagrams parading across the bodies.

Not all of these victims were junkies first—I was sure of it. There had to be more to this story.

The new crime-scene pictures and the reports had been in the mail drop the department had arranged. I assumed the captain had them sent to me so I would have all the information I might need.

And maybe to remind me what I was dealing with.

Like I could forget.

# Chapter 3

"Can I get you something to drink?" the bartender asked. I leaned against the bar in the blood house, my sleeve brushing Reese's. Only three nights had passed since the first visit, and once again I was wired, Iverson and his crew listening in. Garrett had walked in with me, but I hadn't seen where he'd headed next. I was trying not to think about it.

"A glass of the house Shiraz," Reese said.

"With or without?" The bartender sounded bored. He couldn't have been more than nineteen or twenty. I didn't think he was a vampire, and I didn't see any scars—but I didn't understand how a human could work here, night after night.

Maybe he liked the rush of danger.

Or maybe he didn't acknowledge his own mortality.

A small smile played around the edges of Reese's mouth. "Without, please."

Or maybe I didn't understand vampires yet.

"You?" The bartender turned to me.

"Cranberry juice, please." I wasn't about to risk getting drunk.

"With or without?"

I looked at Reese questioningly.

"Without," he said. The bartender nodded and turned to fill our orders.

I leaned toward Reese, tilting in close enough that the brim of his black felt cowboy hat shaded me from the harsh light of the glittering chandelier. "Without what?" I asked.

"Blood." One corner of his mouth crooked up as he waited for my response.

"Oh, God." Even though I'd been whispering, my voice echoed into a momentary lull in the conversations surrounding us. I lowered it. "That's nasty."

Reese grinned. "Actually, darlin', it's pretty damn tasty. And it serves as both a drink and a meal." His drawl was out in full force.

I swallowed convulsively.

"Well," Reese said, the crooked lip deepening into a full-blown grin, "I guess it's a good thing for both of us that I ordered our drinks 'without.' I'd hate for you to cause a scene."

The bartender handed me my glass and I took a sip. But not until after I had examined the drink, the glass, and the rim of the glass for any bloody remains.

Reese leaned back against the bar, one booted foot propped up on the base of the barstool next to him, one hand propped in his pants pocket, and took a sip of his wine.

"So what do you need to know?" Reese asked.

I matched his stance, lowering my voice and checking to make sure no one was listening. Apparently, our little show two nights ago had diverted any suspicion—exactly as it was meant to—leaving us free to talk more or less openly. "A rogue vamp, killing humans. Leaving the bodies in carefully arranged poses."

"So I've heard," said Reese. "Arranged in star-shaped configurations?"

I blinked. "Some of them. What else do you know?"

He pursed his lips as he looked around the room, watching for something he apparently didn't see.

"We need any information you have," I pressed. "The Vamp Admin isn't talking to us—and that makes it seem like they have something to hide."

"I don't know anything definite yet." He shrugged, most of his attention still on scanning the room.

I sipped my drink and changed tactics, determined to get more information from the vampire. "Can you really introduce me to the local admins?"

"Definitely." His gaze settled on something on the other side of the room, and his voice grew clipped. "Get ready. We're up." I mustered up the courage to take another drink of my cranberry juice, forcing myself not to turn around to find out what had caught his eye.

I didn't have to wait long. A tall man moved up to the bar, shouldering his way in between us. His short, thick hair was mostly dark, but silvered at the temples. Silvery glints highlighted the rest of his hair, as well. Laugh lines crinkled the edges of his eyes and creased the corners of his mouth.

After the bartender handed him his drink, he turned and tipped his glass toward me in acknowledgment before taking a sip. From the viscous smear the dark red drink left as it slid back to the bottom of the glass, I could tell that this man had ordered his drink "with."

I swirled the juice in my glass, staring down at it.

Strange. I wouldn't have pegged him for a vampire.

He looked too…the word that came to mind was *distinguished*, but as I looked around, I realized that what I really meant was *old*.

On the whole, vampires were young—or at least, young at the time of their death and subsequent un-death. I mean, that was part of the allure, right? Die now; stay young forever.

In three years on the Sucker Squad, I had never seen a vamp who had been turned after his or her late thirties, tops. They were narcissistic; they liked others just like them: young, beautiful, and amoral.

I glanced back up from my drink at the older vampire and realized he had engaged Reese in quiet conversation. I leaned toward them, intending to join their discussion. I didn't get very far, though, because a pair of hands clamped down on my shoulder.

"Hey, baby," a male voice whispered in my ear. His words slurred a bit and his breath carried the copper stench of blood, overlaid with the astringent smell of alcohol.

*Can a vampire get drunk?* I wondered. It was my last coherent thought for the moment because just then he sank his fangs into my neck, above the opposite shoulder from my Reese-born wounds.

My yelp of pain brought Reese's attention to me, but before he could even move my police training took over. I stomped on the vampire's instep then twisted out of his grip. His teeth ripped through my skin with a tearing, searing pain.

And then my world slowed down as it always does in a fight, my idiosyncratic reaction to adrenaline coursing through my body.

I felt the blood well up in the new wound. The air brushed cold against it as the blood slowly fell to the ground in huge, splashing drops that were slung out to the side as I spun. I grabbed the vampire's hand, twisted his arm up behind his back, and pushed him to the floor, holding him down with my knees in the center of his back, my hand resting on the stake in the holster at the small of my back.

So there I was, kneeling on the back of a vampire in a blood house. With lots of other vampires in the room. Most of them, it seemed, were standing around me in a big, ugly vampire circle. And some of them were hissing.

*Not a pupil to be seen,* I thought as I stared up into the ring of glowing blue eyes. *I'm about to die. And I think I've blown my cover. Oh, fuck.*

My gaze flickered from vampire to vampire, finally settling on Reese. He nodded once and stepped toward me, turning to make eye contact with each of the vampires surrounding us.

"This one is mine." His voice echoed into the suddenly silent room. Without looking at me, he waved two fingers in a downward, slicing motion.

My cue.

Maybe we could salvage this operation after all.

I pulled the stake from the holster, and with one quick, jabbing motion, I slammed it through the downed vampire's back and into his heart.

Three years on the Sucker Squad, and I still wasn't used to how easily the wood penetrated through whatever it is that leaves vampires impervious to other weapons.

I always feel it when the life force leaves a vampire, and this time was no different. The almost electric shock shuddered up the stake and into my hand right as I ripped the wood out of his back.

"She's mine," Reese said again as a few of the vampires hissed. He reached back to grab me by the arm and hauled me up to my feet so that I stood with my back against his chest. "I Claim her. He tried to bleed her without my permission. This kill is mine."

The older-looking vampire took a step forward and surveyed our little tableau. His nostrils flared.

"No," he said.

No? What did he mean? I turned my face up to Reese's, eyes wide. Reese didn't look at me. Instead, he raised one eyebrow at the vampire.

"No?" Reese repeated. He spoke more slowly now, his voice a deep, almost mocking drawl.

"She may indeed be yours, but you have not Claimed her." The older-looking vampire's nostrils flared even wider, and he closed his eyes as he breathed in deeply. "In fact," he said, "you haven't bled her at all tonight. I'd be surprised if she's been bled more than once, maybe twice, in the last week. She'd be worth it, though."

Taking a deep breath, I resecured my grip on the stake.

The older-looking vampire smiled at me. It deepened the creases around his eyes and mouth and actually made him even more attractive. He reached into his pocket and pulled out a white handkerchief. I watched him warily as he reached out and placed it gently against the wound on my neck. I nodded my thanks and pressed against the fabric, but kept the hand with the stake free.

With a slight smile, he stepped back, moving out of my personal space.

"However," he said to Reese, "I think that we'll allow you to claim the kill. On one condition." He waggled his finger to include both of us in his condition. "You must come back to my office and explain why you would assert a Claim that has not been made."

"Your office?" I asked. "Here?"

The vampire nodded, amusement sparkling behind his gaze as he watched me put together the pieces.

"Who are you?" I asked.

"How remiss of me." He reached out and took my right hand, completely ignoring the stake in my grasp as he raised it to his lips in an old-fashioned, courtly gesture. "My dear, I own this blood house. You may call me Don Mendoza."

"Mendoza," I repeated. "Administrator Mendoza?"

The Mendoza who ran all of Dallas had just seen me kill a vampire? Oh, shit. *Was* my cover intact? I watched the administrator carefully for any sign that my takedown had set off alarms.

Mendoza raised his voice so it could be heard throughout the blood house. "This bloodgiver has passed my test. The kill is Claimed. She is protected by Reese, and you are not to touch her without permission."

Passed his test? The administrator of Dallas had set a vampire on me as a test?

Iverson's voice echoed in my ear. "Damn. Cami, you need to get out of there."

Mendoza raised his eyebrows at the sound of Iverson's voice and gripped my hand tighter. His nostrils flared again. "Indeed."

# Chapter 4

We followed Administrator Mendoza back past the bar and through another red-velvet-curtained division. He led us to a hallway with several doors on the right-hand side and opened the first of these doors. I glanced nervously over at Reese, but he neither answered me nor returned my look. He simply took off his cowboy hat and tapped it against his leg.

"My dear," Mendoza said, turning to me, "I will need you to remove your surveillance equipment. I do hope you understand." He glanced at Reese, shaking his head in mock sadness. "I do not understand why you attempt to gain information by subterfuge when you know it will not work."

*He thinks Reese arranged for the bug? Small favors.*

Without taking his eyes off of the administrator, Reese tilted his head in my direction. "Take off the wire, Cami."

My hands shook as I reached up and pulled out the earpiece, offering it to the administrator. He gestured behind us, where a large, muscular vampire waited. "Please give them to Jorge."

Jorge took the equipment and Mendoza ushered us into his office. Reese placed one hand on the small of my back as we moved through the doorway. I found the contact strangely comforting.

Mendoza's office looked much like the rest of the blood house—red and black with lots of velvet. He had a definite theme going here. I wondered in passing how he managed to get blood out of velvet.

*I bet his cleaning bill is enormous.*

I checked the handkerchief Mendoza had given me, and then reached up to gingerly explore the tear in my neck. Although blood had soaked through the cloth, the wound itself had stopped bleeding. I considered offering the handkerchief back to Mendoza, but opted instead to tuck it in a pocket.

The administrator ignored the desk and sat down on an old-fashioned sofa, leaving two wingback chairs for us. All upholstered in dark red velvet. Of course. He crossed his legs and brushed what I suspected was imaginary lint from his pant leg before looking up at us and steepling his fingers under his chin.

"So," he said. "Why are you here?" His dark eyes caught mine, and I could feel myself desperately wanting to tell him everything. I clamped my teeth together so hard my jaw ached.

*Reese can do the talking.*

I tore my eyes away from Mendoza's and stared at the carpet. It was clearly expensive. Probably antique Persian. I focused all of my attention on the red and black design.

"We're here for an evening of entertainment," Reese said mildly.

"With surveillance equipment? I think not. Look at me." I knew without a doubt that Mendoza was talking to me. Against my will, my gaze dragged up from the carpet and moved up over his feet, then legs, then torso, until it reached his face. But by dint of absolute will, I was able to focus on his left cheek. I knew that if I looked into his eyes, I'd be unable to resist him. And then I might tell him everything I knew. And not only about vampires, either. He'd probably get several years' worth of past case information too.

Reese reached over and put his hand on my forearm. I realized that I was clutching the arms of the chair. But with the touch, I relaxed my iron hold a little.

Odd, the effect Reese had on me.

Though my eyes were firmly focused on Mendoza's cheek, I could still see him frown. I could also see what I hadn't noticed before: His skin wasn't the extreme shade of pale I had come to expect from vampires. It had an ashy tint to it, as if he had been darker at one point and that darkness had faded out, not to white, but to a drab khaki.

"So there is a connection between you two after all," said Mendoza. "Interesting." He made that creepy vamp sniffing motion again. "You really should truly bleed her. Let me know if she is as intoxicating as her smell indicates."

I felt more of Mendoza's control over me slip away. I wasn't sure if it was because of Reese's help, or because Mendoza had let go voluntarily, or if somehow my own irritation at his words made me more able to resist him. I didn't much care at that point. I was simply glad to be able to breathe again. I peeled my arms up off the chair and folded them across my chest, then ripped my gaze away from Mendoza's face and watched Reese instead.

"As I said, I've Claimed her." That I found Reese's pronouncement comforting highlighted just how dangerous this situation was becoming.

"But not in the usual way of such things," Mendoza said.

"No." Reese offered no more information, instead letting that half-smile of his flicker briefly into existence.

Mendoza's eyes narrowed to suspicious slits. "So how is it that she, not Claimed, is still yours?"

Reese shook his head and smiled. "Not a chance, chief. You get blood your way; I get it mine." He leaned back in his chair and kicked one leg up over the other so that his ankle rested on the knee of the opposite leg. Across from him, Mendoza looked positively prim with his legs crossed at the thigh, his chiseled face serious beneath his silvered locks.

Mendoza tapped his forefingers together then touched them against his pursed lips as he studied both of us.

"And yet," he said to Reese, "you come here often. Your"—he paused and separated his hands so that he could flick his long, thin fingers in my direction—"pet has not been with you on those occasions."

"It's still a new relationship." The curl of Reese's lip, the deepening of his voice, the slight pause before the word *relationship,* all served to make the words sound as if they described something not only dirty, but utterly depraved.

I shook my head, still fighting off the lingering effects of Mendoza's mind-control game. I got the feeling that Reese had gained the upper hand somehow, but I wasn't entirely certain why. Clearly, Mendoza thought there was more to our alliance than actually existed.

Now Reese was the one picking imaginary lint off his pants. "I'll tell you what. You let us walk out of here, and we won't ever come back. I don't have much interest in spending my time someplace where Claims aren't honored." He looked up and met Mendoza's eyes squarely.

I might not know much about vampire etiquette, but even I could tell that Reese's comment was a slur.

Mendoza uncrossed his legs and leaned forward slightly.

"I don't think that will be necessary," he said. "By all means, please feel free to return. And be assured that I will see to it that all Claims—even such, shall we say, unconventional ones—are honored."

Reese nodded once. "Thank you, sir. Much obliged." He nodded again, placed his hat on his head, touched the brim, and held his hand out to me. I stood up, once again glad for his steadying touch.

I turned to follow Reese out, but at the last minute, he turned back toward Mendoza.

"Sanguinary," he said, and I stumbled to a stop behind him, trying to gauge Mendoza's reaction without looking directly at his face. I couldn't tell much—he might have frozen in place at the word, but he might simply be doing that vampire-still thing. "I still want in."

One corner of the administrator's mouth turned up. "Of course you do. These things cannot be rushed." He gestured in a clear dismissal.

He didn't speak to us again, but followed us as far as the door to speak to Jorge, who stood guard in the hall. "Please see that this gentleman and his bloodgiver are treated respectfully tonight."

Jorge nodded and motioned us down the hall in front of him.

As we moved through the curtain and back into the main room, I clutched Reese's arm.

"What was that?" I whispered furiously.

"Later," he said.

I realized that the guard was still watching us, albeit from a respectful distance—but I didn't know how acute a vampire's hearing might be.

"We need to leave now," I whispered.

"Not yet." Reese spoke in his normal voice. He sounded dismissive. I hoped that was for the sake of anyone who might be listening in. I felt my blood boil at his dismissal, despite the risk.

In the fifteen minutes we'd spent in Mendoza's office, the dead vampire's body had been cleared away. In fact, all signs of struggle had been wiped out. Or wiped up, more likely, since the vampire had probably leaked blood onto the floor. And I had a vague recollection of slinging my drink across the room when I spun to grab the vamp.

Then again, I suspected that these people were used to cleaning up disgusting red liquid messes.

The memory of the struggle hadn't been wiped away, though. Everyone stared at us as we made our way back up to the bar. I stuck as close to Reese as possible without actually plastering my body up against his. I didn't entirely trust Mendoza's bodyguard to protect me if the vampires surrounding me suddenly decided to attack.

A space cleared for us as if by magic.

It occurred to me that there might be some benefit to being known as a vampire killer, after all.

I was going to need a drink—a real one this time.

But Reese had other ideas. With one hand, he grasped my upper arm so tightly it felt like the circulation had been cut off. Staring over my head and scanning the room for anyone who got too close, he whispered harshly, "How did you resist Mendoza's mind control?"

"You're hurting me," I said through gritted teeth.

His grip tightened. "Smile and talk."

I felt my heart rate pick up. I'd be wise to remember that Reese was one of them. Garrett had said Reese was on our side, as much as it was possible for any vamp to be. But he still might not think of us as anything more than dinner.

I scolded myself for letting his cowboy hat and dimpled smile— not to mention his meltingly hot body—lead me to forget that he was every bit as much a monster as any other vampire in the room. His hold on my arm reminded me forcibly of that fact now.

"Do you want to discuss it here?" I was playing for time, really. I'd left my surveillance equipment with Jorge, so Iverson probably wasn't coming any time soon—I didn't see him calling in the troops after he heard me willingly hand over the gear. And for all I knew, Jorge had completely forgotten about it, and Iverson was right this minute learning all the secrets of the Vampire Administration.

Reese loosened his hold enough for my circulation to recover, the blood rushing to my palm like needles dancing across it. I rubbed it with the thumb of my other hand, and Reese's gaze followed the motion.

"We're leaving," he said, his voice harsh.

*No. No way in hell am I walking out of here with a pissed-off vampire.*

That was how cops ended up dead.

I took a step backwards and pulled myself up onto a barstool, reaching for my own willpower to stall him. Reese's upper lip curled, revealing a fang, and I held out my hands placatingly. "Hear me out."

It hit me, hard, that no matter how I twisted it around in my head, Reese was going to be more than just an informant to me. I didn't know if I could trust him, this cowboy-vampire I had been thrown together with. But something about him sang to me, like a tune just out of hearing, almost recognized—a song of protection and death. And I wanted to dance to it, almost as much as I wanted to escape it.

The department wouldn't force me to stick it out, wouldn't expect me to team up with a vampire for anything more than the most superficial of connections.

It helped to know I could walk out at any time.

But I also knew I wouldn't.

I was certain that Reese would help us find and stop whoever was killing these women.

*That's why I'll stay in this.*

"I'll tell you everything," I said to the vampire snarling at me. "But I'll need your help."

Reese's lip dropped back down, covering the fang.

I was glad—it was easier to contemplate joining forces with him when he wasn't reminding me that he was one of the monsters.

"Talk," he said.

I shook my head. "Not here." I spoke quietly. How good his hearing might be was only one of the many things I didn't know about vampires.

He slid up to the bar beside me.

"We can't leave," he replied, equally softly. I had to lean close to hear him.

"Why not?" I asked.

"Mendoza all but dared me to Claim you, back there." He didn't look down at me. "If I don't bleed you at least a little before we go, he'll be suspicious."

At his words, the half-healed bite mark Reese had left on my shoulder throbbed once, sending a hot pulse throughout my entire body.

I wanted the response to be revulsion.

Almost everyone who went undercover with the vamps came out addicted to their bite. The ones who could still string two sentences together, like Garrett, stayed on the force.

The others...

The press portrayed the police as bumbling and stupid—and maybe we were. Sending detectives in against humanity's worst nightmare? We were like little kids trying to hold back the dark with matches, bound to get our fingers burned, and worse, maybe burn the house down around us.

I paused and swallowed.

The wound left by the other vampire—the one I had killed—didn't respond at all, making me wonder if there was something more than just the physiological at work.

I took a long, ragged breath. "Okay," I said. "Whatever we need to do."

He glanced down at me now. "Anything?"

I shuddered, my nipples suddenly hardening beneath the light silk of the camisole I wore. "Anything necessary," I clarified.

His nostrils flared at the same time his lips parted slightly, and I knew he was tasting my desire on the air around us.

With a nod, he took my hand and tugged me gently off the barstool, leading us both back toward the curtained alcoves.

My heart raced in my chest, but I fought to keep my breath even. As we moved into the small room, another tremor shook me.

Part of me was terrified of the possibility that Reese was using the blood house meet as a chance to get a free meal.

The rest of me wanted his touch so badly it didn't matter why he was doing it.

I had to keep that second, larger part of myself in check.

"So what's with the public bloodletting?" I asked, proud that my voice didn't shake. "Why not do this in the privacy of your own homes?"

Reese sat on the couch, pulling me down next to him. "Two reasons," he said. "The first is community restraint. If a vampire loses control, we can take him or her down before the human dies."

"And that's important to you?"

He nodded. "Very. We live here, too—it's no good for any of us if one vampire sets the whole city against us. And we like our food alive."

Then why wasn't the administration talking to us about the vamp murders? Why wouldn't they want the killer caught?

"And the second reason?" I asked, choosing not to bring up the killings.

"It's a bad idea to let humans know where we sleep. A business like this allows us the privacy we prefer for these kinds of things, but is public enough to help keep everyone safe—including the humans, who aren't compelled to invite us into their homes."

I sat silent for a long moment, contemplating a world where vampires bled their victims dry on a regular basis, or tore them to shreds in their own homes. A world where humans went on a citywide hunt for the monsters that were killing them.

Was that the kind of world the perpetrator of the vamp murders wanted to create?

The laws, spoken and unspoken, made just a little more sense. I shivered again, but this time there was no desire in the tremble. "I don't know how I resisted Mendoza earlier. But when you touched me, it was easier to hold him at bay."

Reese nodded thoughtfully. "I wondered if it might."

We sat together without speaking, and for the first time, I felt almost comfortable with him.

"Let's get this over with," I finally said, pulling the collar of my shirt aside and baring my neck to Reese. I didn't trust him—not really, not yet—but no one else was around, and I had no choice but to do this.

"First," he whispered, "let me help you." He licked his thumb and ran it across the wound the other vampire had left. A tingling, burning sensation followed his touch, and when I reached up to check the bite, I felt the hard edges of a scab—the kind that shouldn't be there for days, at least, or maybe longer.

I opened my mouth to ask about it, but Reese shook his head and placed his fingertip across my lips.

My heart stuttered as he bent down and slid his tongue gently across the recent wounds he had created, drawing a line of fire between the two puncture marks. Then he traced another line with his tongue up a little higher on my neck, following the vein. With a sigh, I closed my eyes, and he sank his fangs into me.

It shouldn't have felt so much like coming home.

# Chapter 5

I needed to remember where this assignment could end. After all, Garrett hadn't always been a vamp addict. When I first joined the Sucker Squad, he had been my mentor as well as my partner. Then he went undercover for six months, and when he came out, he was a shadow of the gruff, plainspoken man who had trained me.

I might have been able to better handle Garrett's vampire-addiction problem if I hadn't seen it in action, first-hand. But finding him in that basement had rammed home the fact that he was really and truly a junkie.

Still, I had wanted to protect him from the repercussions of that addiction, since it developed in the department's service.

I'd almost left out his basement splurge from my official report all those months ago. I even considered convincing Jeanie to keep quiet.

In the end, though, I was too well trained to keep Garrett's problem to myself.

I included everything and filed the report.

And apparently he was still worth something to the force—otherwise, the brass wouldn't have kept him on.

It was the next day—after we'd taken the vamp-addled Garrett home and cleaned him up, and I'd gone back to the precinct to write my report—that Lieutenant Iverson had stuck his blond, buzz-cut head out of his office and called me over. "Captain wants to see you in his office."

I nodded and headed down the hall.

I didn't know what I anticipated, but I wasn't expecting to glance through the windows into Captain James's office and see the chief of police.

"He'll be with you in a minute," Stacy, Captain James's secretary, said. I took a seat and waited, a little surprised by how anxious I felt.

A few minutes later, Chief Wallace Paige left the office. A large, quiet, black man with graying sideburns, he always looked serious, as if he was taking in the scene around him and noticing every detail. The kind of man I would want to have my back in a dangerous situation.

Right now, he looked like a man dropped down unexpectedly into the middle of that danger. Every line of his body radiated tension.

"Detective Davis." He nodded at me as he passed.

He knew who I was, and presumably why I was there.

*This is not good.*

I waited a few minutes longer. Andre Perricone, the latest addition to the Sucker Squad, came in and dropped an envelope on Stacy's desk, hanging around a few extra minutes to flirt with the secretary.

*He looks so young.*

Only three years in, and already I felt jaded.

The phone on Stacy's desk buzzed and she picked it up, murmuring a few words. "You can go in," she said to me.

Captain James didn't look up as I walked in.

"Shut the door behind you."

He continued staring at the crime-scene photos on his desk in front of him.

"Have a seat."

As I waited, he pushed the photos around with one forefinger.

"Fifty years," he finally said, after a long, silent moment.

"Sir?" I leaned forward to see if I could piece together what he meant. The photos were from the last two crime scenes—the ones staged by the perp the uniforms had already started calling the Vamp Killer, though to be honest, at that point we weren't entirely certain a vampire had done the killing.

"That's how long we've got." He began piling the 8x10s, one on top of the other, in no apparent order. "Fifty years."

"Until what?" I asked.

He tapped the photos into a neat stack, set them aside, and leaned forward, placing his elbows on his desk and clasping his hands in front of him. "Fifty years until we're all either vamps or food."

I suddenly couldn't feel my hands. "According to whom?"

He shrugged, not breaking eye contact with me. "All the experts. I could show you the reports. They're marked *top secret*, but I guarantee there's a copy somewhere in the police district of every major city in the country."

I felt shocky, alternating between too hot and too cold, but I didn't disbelieve him for even a second.

"The bastards are organized, Davis—and sneaky as hell. We don't know anything about them, and they know everything about us. Nine years in, and we've already lost."

Almost ten years, actually, since vampires had come rising up out of the darkness all over the world, claiming they'd always been here.

But they didn't have an explanation for revealing themselves—at least, not one they gave to us. Best anyone could figure, they had waited until there were enough vamps that they had a chance of winning if it turned to all-out war.

It hadn't. Not yet. Not quite.

Perhaps unsurprisingly, there were conspiracy theorists, people who claimed that vampires weren't what they said they were—that they were from a different dimension, or were aliens from another world.

I didn't really care where they came from, as long as they didn't go around killing innocent humans. And they didn't have to kill the ones they fed from.

But they liked killing.

It had been intensely bloody for a few years as we humans had learned to fight back, had relearned that stakes and beheading and the cleansing fire of sunlight were our friends.

We thought we were winning this not-yet-war. Or at least, I had. Sure, there might be the occasional rogue vampire killing for the fun of it, like the psycho taking out women in Dallas right now. But there were more of us, and as evidenced by my experience at the blood house, the vampires preferred truce, too.

But there was also a good chance it was only our superior numbers keeping the vampires from openly declaring war on us.

And if they were building up their numbers…

*Fifty years. Oh, dear God.*

"That's why I'm going to be sending you undercover," James said. "We don't have any other choice. We have to get someone on the inside, and Garrett's the cleanest insert we've got."

An image of my partner begging the vampire not to leave him flashed through my mind.

There was nothing clean about that.

I blinked the mental picture away and spoke tentatively. "I've been on the Sucker Squad for three years, sir. Won't the vampires know who I am?"

"Maybe. But from what we can tell, we only ever catch the least important vamps." He shrugged, one shoulder hitching up around his shirt collar. "And honestly? Even the times we're sure they've known we were working to place agents among them, they simply don't seem to care."

We were definitely in trouble. But I had to try.

God help me, I actually thought, *Garrett can handle a basic introduction to a vampire contact.*

That was all he was supposed to do: get me in, then get him out.

The best laid plans, and all that.

# Chapter 6

"So tell me what you know about Sanguinary," I said to Reese. We stood in the shadowed arch of a doorway a few blocks away from the blood house. It was close to midnight. I barely remembered having stumbled out of the house, hanging from Reese's arm, reeling like a drunkard on the tail end of a three-day bender.

And that was after only a slight bleeding.

Reese opened the bottle of orange juice he had insisted we stop and get from the convenience store at the other end of the street. He handed it to me, and I took a long drink. He apparently wanted me refreshed. Healthy.

Peering past the recessed doorway, Reese scouted the area around us. When he saw no one coming from any direction, he spoke. "It's a group of vampires, a small contingent. But powerful and growing. They don't want to integrate with humans—or rather, they think that any integration should be in the form of changing humans to vampires."

"So they're dangerous. Typical vamps," I said, almost snarkily.

He stared intently into my eyes. "We're all monsters."

I didn't rise to the bait. "More than usually dangerous, then?"

With another glance around the empty street, Reese nodded. "Although I don't know for sure, my guess is that they're behind the murders you're here to solve. I don't think it's a rogue vampire at all. I think it's the whole group of them, either doing the killing themselves, or at least giving the orders. They're gaining more and more power, and I want them taken down."

I paused, momentarily sidetracked by a stray thought. "Why call themselves the 'Sanguinary'? Other than the blood connection, I mean."

He shrugged. "It means both bloody and bloodthirsty, so I guess it fits."

"How long has the group been around? Why are they showing up now?" I asked.

"I don't know." He took his cowboy hat off and tapped it against his leg—a movement I was beginning to recognize as a sign of agitation. "They were around before I was turned."

I was missing something here—something that Reese was hiding—but I didn't know enough to ask the right questions. So I asked what I could.

"How long ago was that?" I didn't know if it was rude to ask a vampire his age, but I wasn't going to let vamp propriety stop me.

"Eight years." Pointing at the half-empty orange juice bottle in my hand, he raised his eyebrows. "Finish that. We need to go."

Eight years.

I didn't know of a single vampire who had been around before they all showed up a little over ten years ago. None of the Sucker Squad files mentioned any elder vampires—not that the humans knew about, anyway, not outside of fiction.

Fifty years before we were all under the vampires' control, unless someone could learn enough to stop it.

The knowledge that the vampires had not really been around before ten years ago was a piece of solving that puzzle, I was sure. Did the Sanguinary include the older vampires who were rumored to exist?

My instinct told me I was on the right track.

I needed to give Jeanie a call to find out if they'd gotten DNA back from the Winspear scene. I wanted to find out if the slip of paper that said *Sanguinary* on it had been in the victim's blood. Had the vic known about the group before she was taken? Had that been what had drawn the Sanguinary's attention to her?

I tilted the orange juice up as I swallowed the last of it, then handed the empty back to Reese, who tucked it into a pocket.

"Okay. What can you find out?" I asked.

He glanced up at the sky, as if he could judge the hours until daylight without a watch. "Give me a couple of nights—I'll keep politicking for entrance. Having you as my bloodgiver will help with that, I think."

An unwelcome tremor ran through me at the words. I looked straight ahead and ignored it, along with the tiny voice in the back of my head that suggested he hadn't told me much that I hadn't already known. "What's next?"

"I'll be in touch either tomorrow or the next night," he finally said.

"And what should I do in the meantime?" I asked.

Reese reached out with one finger and brushed it against the collar of my shirt. "Laundry, maybe?"

I followed his gaze down to where he had touched me and found two small, round bloodstains marring the fabric above the spot where his fangs had slid into me earlier.

I shrugged his hand off of me and stalked out of the alcove, ignoring both the way my nipples sprang to attention at the memory of the bloodletting and the dark chuckle I heard behind me.

# Chapter 7

By the time I got to the street where I had parked my car, I could no longer see Reese.

But I sensed his presence, watching to make sure no one bothered me on the dark and empty sidewalk.

I couldn't decide how I felt about that.

Iverson was waiting by my car when I got there—I assumed the van was somewhere nearby, as well.

"You okay?" he asked.

I unlocked and opened my car door, shaking my head. "I can tell you care by the way you rushed in to save me back there when Mendoza took my gear."

He had the good grace to look uncomfortable.

"Look, I understand." My voice was tired. "We need to know what I can find out more than we need any one cop. Just tell me: Did you hear anything else once I handed over the equipment?"

"No," he said, seemingly thankful to turn the discussion to a more businesslike topic. "They disabled it pretty quickly. Captain wants you to send in a report tomorrow. Leave it at the mail drop."

I blew a breath out and swung myself into the driver's seat. "I'll see what I can do. I've got some laundry to take care of first."

In my rearview mirror, I could see Iverson standing in the street staring after me all the way to the corner as I drove away.

* * *

By noon the next day, I had washed not only the shirt I'd been wearing the night before, but every piece of clothing I owned.

I had spent the rest of the previous evening putting together a report confirming the Sanguinary connection to the murders and had left it in the mail drop early that morning.

It was a relief to focus on the simple, homey task of laundry.

Having finished the last load for the day, I was trotting up the stairs from the first-floor laundry room, basket in hand. I hadn't been out for a run in several days and was beginning to be able to tell. Even this jog up the stairs left me slightly breathless. Tomorrow, I promised myself. Tomorrow I'd hit the gym.

I felt so damned tired. I was beginning to suspect that might come with being a bloodgiver.

Wrapped up in my own thoughts, I didn't notice the man standing in the shadows of the stairway a few doors down.

He saw me, though. It was clear he was waiting for me. As I balanced the basket on my knee with my elbow and used the other hand to unlock the apartment, he moved toward me, and that was when I saw him.

I took a moment to scan him as he approached, hands in pockets. Dark hair, tan skin, dark suit. Sunglasses—probably a Ray-Ban knockoff, though I couldn't really tell the difference between fakes and the real things. When he got close enough to speak, he took the sunglasses off.

"Detective Davis?" he asked, his voice polite but professional.

Definitely a Fed.

"Just Cami, these days," I replied, working to keep my voice neutral. If the Feds were working with the Sucker Squad right now, no one had told me about it.

"Cami, then," he said. "Can I talk with you for a moment?"

"ID?" I asked.

He pulled it out and flashed it at me, then passed it over when I propped the basket on my hip and held out my hand.

Yep. FBI.

"Okay, Agent Stan Chandler." I handed his badge back to him. "Come on in."

I didn't look back as I moved inside, but I could hear him following me as I dropped the basket on a chair. I kept moving, through the small living room and around the counter separating it from the kitchen. "Water?" I asked, opening the refrigerator and pulling out a couple of bottles.

He took one from me. "Thanks. It's hot out there."

"So," I said, after I took a long swig from my own bottle, "what can I help you with?" I leaned my hip against the counter.

"I was wondering if you could talk to me about the blood house."

I took another drink. "Blood house?" I moved toward the living room to give myself time to think. He was watching me too carefully; I didn't want him to see me considering his words. "What do you want to know?" I asked, sitting down on the couch. He followed my lead, lowering himself onto the loveseat across from me and leaning forward, his expression open.

It was a technique I had used before—it made suspects feel comfortable, as if we were merely two friends chatting.

Fat chance.

"I want to know why your chief has you checking it out," Chandler said, his voice still calm. "I want to know what you've learned."

I shook my head. "I think you've got your wires crossed, Agent. I don't know if you've heard, but I'm no longer with the force."

He snorted—not the kind of sound I expected to hear from an FBI agent. "You know, if it turns out that Felicia Monroe made it to Louisiana—if there's any evidence of the killer crossing state lines—we could make it a federal case."

He leaned toward me, elbows on his knees and hands clasped loosely, trying far too hard to look casual.

"In fact," he said, dropping his voice, "as soon as we're sure the doer is a vamp, we can take over the case."

Time to shift the topic, at least a little bit. Leaning back, I swallowed the rest of my water in one long gulp. "Not my department anymore." I shrugged. "Maybe the FBI should take over the case. Doesn't look like the Dallas PD is getting anywhere."

Chandler leaned back, stretching one arm out along the back of the couch and crossing one ankle over his knee. "Maybe so."

"I really don't have anything to tell you. My former partner is introducing me around the vamp scene. I need a job, and the vampires need…" I paused suggestively. "Well, they need all kinds of things." I crooked up one corner of my mouth. "I don't know if I'll go back to the blood house." Forcing myself to lean back, to look relaxed, I tilted my head at the agent. "But I'm sure you'd be popular. They seem to like the clean-cut type."

That got a response, though I'm not sure I would have noticed the shiver that ran down his back if I hadn't been watching as carefully as I was.

"So you haven't learned anything about the Sanguinary?" he asked. His voice was much calmer than that shudder would have led me to expect—it was as if he hadn't had any reaction at all.

My heart, on the other hand, sped up. I was glad Chandler wasn't a vampire, because he probably would have picked up on the response. As it was, though, I kept my expression blank.

"Sanguinary?" I asked. "Not a clue."

He stared at me for a long time, trying to make me nervous, to force me to fill the quiet. But I was a pro, too—he wasn't going to break me with silence. I let it go on long enough to make most people uncomfortable, then took a breath as if I were about to speak. I blew it out and leaned forward to put my empty water bottle on the coffee table in front of me.

"You might consider checking in with the local police," I said. "If there's anything illegal going on at the blood house, I certainly didn't see it. Other than the usual vampirism, of course." I blinked at him. "Maybe I could write down Captain James's information for you." I mustered the most innocent tone I could manage. "Or perhaps Chief Wallace? They'll certainly have more information than I do these days." I stood and gestured toward the door. "Now, if you don't mind, I have some errands to run."

Agent Chandler rose and reached into his pocket. "Let me know if you think of anything?" He held out a business card "And could you please tell your partner, Mr. Garrett, that I'm looking for him?"

I shook my head. "I'm sorry. We're not partners. I haven't talked to him since he introduced me around the blood house."

"If you do hear from them, then." He pressed the card into my hand, and I took it.

"Of course." I smiled as I ushered him outside, then started to close the door, but he stopped it with his palm.

"And Ms. Davis?" he said. "I don't believe you." He pulled his sunglasses back over his eyes, nodded at me, and walked away. The Feds were working the Sanguinary angle too. If Chandler got too close, he could blow my cover. I needed to let Iverson know that other agencies were nosing around.

I glanced down at the cell phone—the new one, the one that only Reese and the department had access to—sitting on the end table by my couch and chewed lightly on my bottom lip. I was already reaching for it when it rang.

Captain James's voice was cold and hard on the other end of the line. "We think Garrett's in trouble. He checked into some fancy rehab clinic last night, way out of his league. We've got intel that the hospital's a front for the vamps, and something big is going down tonight. We're running a sting, and we need you to come in for it."

Acid churned in my stomach. What the hell had Garrett gotten himself into?

"You think Garrett's in on it?" I tried to sound professional, but a thread of anxiety ran through my voice anyway. "Or is it a way to get rid of him?"

"The vamps put him in there, one way or another. There's no question about it: Either they placed him there or he's there because of their bite." I could practically hear James's shrug over the phone. "Anyway, it doesn't matter why he's there. He's one of ours. We'll take down the clinic, get Garrett out, and get him help."

I couldn't help but feel guilty for my part in the department's decision to send my partner back into a situation that sparked his addiction.

What had happened to him at the blood house after he left with Dahlia and her friend? Had it been so bad that he had felt the need for vampire rehab? Or had the vampires convinced him to go in?

"You can't pull me out of the Sanguinary op," I said, leaning my back against the door as if to keep it closed. "I'm getting close to something important here. If I break cover now, we might never get near the Sanguinary again."

"We'll get you in and back out, no extraction from your current cover necessary." I could picture him ticking items off on his blunt, square fingers. "We need someone who doesn't look like a cop, someone Garrett trusts. Andre Perricone's going in as a patient. We need you to pose as his sister when he checks in, help place some bugs, give us an overview."

"This is a bad idea," I said.

"Agreed. But it's the best we've got."

"Did you know the Feds are nosing around?" I asked.

He sighed. "Chandler hit you up too? I'll talk to the local office, see if I can get his associate deputy director to rein him in." He paused. "In the meantime, though, I'm sending Iverson to pick you up."

It took a couple of hours to get everything ready. Iverson met me at a convenience store a few blocks from my apartment. He said his surveillance team hadn't picked up anyone following me—I wasn't sure the vamps had eyes on me, but it wouldn't have surprised me. Anyway, Iverson's guys said I was clean, so I did my best to tamp down any anxiety. Once I was in the van, I used a new phone— complete, I was assured, with an appropriate background ID—to call Westlake, posing as Andre's sister, and set up an appointment for Andre that afternoon. I was hoping I'd get a glimpse of Garrett while I was in the clinic, if only to let him know we hadn't abandoned him.

Andre's brown eyes regarded me steadily from the front seat. He was the newest, and youngest, member of the team. I didn't know him very well, but I'd seen him flirt with the secretaries—he'd been flirting with Stacy the day I learned that the vamps were winning this secret war. He had a sweet smile. Captain James was right: Andre didn't look like a cop. His eyes weren't hard enough.

I suspected they'd get that way soon enough.

"I'll make sure Garrett's okay," Andre said quietly.

"Thanks." I smiled at him, blinking to hold back tears. I wasn't sure if they were for Garrett, Andre, me...or maybe all of us.

# Chapter 8

Our appointment was at four. Westlake was right outside of Highland Park, and although it's less than twenty minutes away by car, it's about a million miles away from my part of Dallas in every other aspect. At mid-afternoon on a beautiful fall day, women with strollers walked up and down the street. Most of them were obviously nannies, but a few others were equally as clearly stay-at-home mothers, the sorts of women whose husbands made enough money to allow them to live in this posh Dallas neighborhood and still stay home.

As we got out of the car at the clinic, I grabbed Andre's hand and gave it a squeeze—it was the closest I could come to saying thank you without speaking aloud. I hoped if anyone saw it, they would assume I was trying to give reassurance to my brother as he got ready to check into rehab.

We walked up the short walkway. The front door was opened by a uniformed guard. I looked around surreptitiously, trying to spot the cameras that had alerted him to our presence.

There.

One was in a tree to my left, one to my right. And now that I was looking, I saw the glint of a video-camera lens at the top of the door lintel. With only those three, one guard could monitor the entire entrance. And I was guessing there were more unseen cameras. And guards.

This guard didn't say anything, but he nodded to us as he ushered us in. The entryway opened up into a waiting room furnished to look like an old-fashioned sitting room. The couches were long and Victorian-looking and the chairs were wingbacks. A wooden mantel clock sat on an entryway table under an ornate gilt mirror. Everything was upholstered in florals. In a smaller room, it would have been overpowering. Here, it seemed appropriate.

The only giveaway that this was anything other than your rich great-aunt's house was the receptionist sitting at a Queen Anne-style desk in the back corner of the room.

"May I help you?" she asked in a soft but professional voice.

"Yes," I said. "I have an appointment with Dr. Richards. My name is Deborah Carlson."

"Just a moment," the receptionist replied, and picked up the phone. She spoke into it quietly and then hung up. "Please have a seat. The doctor will be with you shortly." She went back to working on something at her computer.

Andre and I sat down on one of the long couches. The cushion was hard and unyielding—nothing that would make you want to linger in this room very long.

We didn't speak, and the only sounds in the room came from the ticking of the clock and the clacking of the receptionist's keyboard. I sat clutching my large black handbag—a Prada knockoff—to my chest, acutely aware of the Ziploc bag full of electronic gear that Iverson had stowed in it earlier. He had given me instructions on possible places to hide it. Looking around the waiting room, I realized that we had been a bit naïve. There wasn't anywhere in this room to hide anything. The chairs all cleared the floor—no flaps of fabric hanging down to conceal anything underneath them. The backs of the couches weren't against walls. There weren't any bookshelves. The rugs were nice and flat.

This room wouldn't work.

A door on the wall opposite the entrance opened and a tall woman stepped through it. She wore a white lab coat over a black pants suit with high-heeled pumps. Real Prada shoes.

"Ms. Carlson, Mr. Carlson. Nice to meet you." She held out her hand for us to shake. "If you'll follow me." She turned back toward what I assumed was her office. "Please hold any calls, Mary," she said to the receptionist as she held the door open.

Dr. Richards had dark, curly hair pulled into a short ponytail at the nape of her neck. Her glasses perched at the end of her nose as she peered over them at us.

"Please, have a seat," she said, gesturing to the two chairs in front of her desk.

She flipped through a file folder. "So, Mr. Carlson, I see that you are planning to enroll for the two-week treatment plan."

Andre rubbed his hands on his blue jeans and stared down at his legs, looking for all the world like a nervous junkie, despite his muscular torso. It was pretty impressive acting. "Yes, ma'am," he muttered.

"And are you enrolling of your own free will?" Dr. Richards asked.

"Yes." He sounded like a sullen teenager. Perfect.

"Okay, then. I have a few papers for you to sign." She went through the paperwork and "Bill Carlson" admitted himself to the Westlake Clinic for Drug and Alcohol Addiction.

"Good," said Dr. Richards. "I'll have someone show you to your room so you can begin unpacking." She was professional but kind sounding. I was having a hard time believing that this woman was in league with the vampires.

"Does he have to go now?" I asked. "Could you show us around the clinic first?"

"I'll be happy to give you a brief tour. You'll have a chance to see your brother again before you leave," Dr. Richards assured me.

She picked up her phone and murmured into the receiver. A moment later a young woman in nurse's scrubs opened the door.

"Bill? You can come with me now."

Andre stood up and walked out of the room behind her.

Dr. Richards stood as well. "Shall we?" she asked. I followed her back out the door and into the reception area again.

"As you can see, there is always a guard at the front door. This is for both our safety and our patients' well-being." She moved to a large window and gestured at the green expanse of lawn outside. "We also have an electric fence surrounding the property."

"I didn't see one when we drove up." I peered out the window.

"It's connected to the bracelets we require all our patients to wear. If they attempt to leave the premises, an invisible laser boundary administers an electric shock and sets off a warning alarm inside the building. It's not enough of a jolt to seriously hurt them, but it certainly keeps them from wanting to try to leave again."

"Kind of like an invisible dog fence." As soon as the words were out of my mouth, I wanted them back—not because of what I'd said, really, but because of the tone I'd used: a little too sarcastic.

She frowned. "We prefer to think of it as a protective measure. We also have a laser alarm system that allows our security officers to monitor any unauthorized attempts to exit or enter the premises."

I needed to change the subject. "I'm glad to hear it. Tell me about the rest of your staff," I said, dropping into the role of concerned sister who wanted to know everything about her brother's rehab center.

"We have psychiatrists, psychologists, MDs, RNs, and nurses' aides on our staff here, along with several volunteers from the local community—at any given time we have at least two fully qualified medical and psychological specialists to help our patients. This means that your brother will always have access to any sort of medical assistance he needs."

While she spoke, we walked down the hall. I watched for Garrett, but so far, I hadn't seen any of the clinic's residents. I was hoping to make sure he was okay.

I shouldn't have counted on him to get himself out of the blood house alone. I should have at least checked on him.

If I couldn't find Garrett, I could at least examine my surroundings for a place to ditch the baggie of bugs in my purse. Nothing. All the doorways lining the hall were closed.

"Excuse me," I said, not quite interrupting, but clearly breaking into her carefully rehearsed spiel. "Do you have a ladies' room I could use?"

"Of course. Down that hall, last door on the right." She pointed to a hall opposite the one we had come in on. That hall had a metal door at the end of it, as well. "We can finish the tour when you get back," she said.

"Thanks." I smiled at her and scurried into the bathroom. It was depressingly institutional: five stalls with dark blue dividers between them and a double sink along the opposite wall. Some effort had been made to cheer the room up—it had a floral wallpaper border along the top of the wall with big blue peonies that matched the stall dividers.

I ducked into one of the stalls and lifted the lid off the toilet tank. Thank God the toilets were the normal kind with tanks, and not the sort that often gets installed in airports and schools—the sort with the automatic flush and no back tank. I flushed the toilet and watched the water drain out of the tank while I fished the Ziploc out of my purse.

I slipped the bag inside the tank and watched the water cover it. Then I replaced the lid, washed and dried my hands, and walked back out of the bathroom and down the hall.

"Sorry about that," I apologized when I got back to Dr. Richards.

"That's fine," she replied. "Do you have any further questions about Westlake?"

"No, not really," I said. "Can I call you if I think of any?"

"Absolutely." She smiled at me. "Let's take you to say good-bye to your brother."

We walked back down into the first hall and Richards knocked gently on a door in the middle. She opened it without waiting for a reply. Andre was standing by one of the two single beds in the room, moving the last stack of T-shirts from his suitcase to the dresser. At my urging, he had packed clothing that he wouldn't particularly mind leaving behind—just in case we didn't have time for him to repack before we left.

"Hey, sis," he said as I walked in behind Richards.

"Hey." I spoke softly. I looked at Richards, hoping she would leave so that I could tell Andre where I'd left the equipment. She smiled at me blandly.

I didn't know what else to do, so I reached out and awkwardly hugged him. Then it hit me.

"Oh, no." I grabbed my pinky with my other hand and stared at it. "I think I might have left my ring by the washbasin in the ladies' room. I'll be right back." I spun around and headed back to the bathroom, hoping Andre would catch the hint.

I stayed in the restroom long enough to give credence to the thought that I might be looking for a piece of lost jewelry. Then I walked back down to Andre's room.

"Find it?" Richards asked as I came in.

"No," I said, knitting my brows. "I must not have put it on this morning. I was in a bit of a rush. But could you keep an eye out for it, just in case?"

"Of course," she said smoothly. "If we're done here?" Her voice trailed off, clearly an indication that Andre and I should finish saying our good-byes.

I hugged him one more time, and then followed Richards down the hall to the front entrance.

"Nice to meet you, Ms. Carlson." She held open the door for me.

Back outside, I slid into the seat of the sports car and took a deep breath. Hands shaking, I started the engine and drove back to the coffee shop where Iverson and Jeanie were waiting. When they saw me enter, they left. I ordered a latte and followed them down the block a few minutes later. Someone from the department would be by to pick up the sports car later.

"So?" asked Iverson when I climbed into the van. "How'd it go?"

"Fine, I think," I said. "I wasn't able to tell him where I'd hidden the equipment, but I think he picked up on the hints I dropped."

Iverson, Jeanie, and I were crowded into the van with two of Iverson's tech guys, who looked remarkably alike in their black jeans and polo shirts, short brown haircuts, and glasses. Mentally, I labeled them Tech One and Tech Two.

"How's the security?" Jeanie asked.

"Pretty tight. Even the low-security wing has some high-tech stuff." I told them about the invisible fence, the cameras, the guards, the alarm.

"Good job," Iverson said. "Let's figure out the rest of it."

He had me sketch out a rough blueprint of the part of the clinic that I had seen, matching it up to the plans on file with the city.

"This is Andre's room." I pointed to one of the squares on the sheet. "I don't know if the rest of the doors lead to patients' rooms—they were all closed—but it's a pretty good bet."

Jeanie nodded. "Anything else?"

"Not really. There are people stationed at every visible entry point in the place, and probably some other places too. And it sounds like they've got a huge medical staff."

"Okay." Jeanie climbed into the driver's seat and headed back toward the clinic. The next property looked like a private home, but the one after that had been converted to a dentist's office. Closed. Perfect. Jeanie killed the lights as we pulled into the driveway and around to the back, to what looked like the old servants' entrance. This was definitely old-money Dallas. With any luck, the dark blue of the van would be virtually invisible at night.

Tech One and Tech Two started fiddling with the controls on their gear. I leaned around the front seat and watched them.

Nothing but static.

It took about another two hours, and then it was only one short burst of a message.

We'd been sitting in the back playing gin rummy with an old deck of cards Jeanie had scrounged from the glove box. We had gotten so used to the white noise of the static in the background that when it suddenly squealed and squelched, Jeanie and I jumped—but not Iverson. He watched, narrow-eyed, as Tech Two clarified the sound.

At first I thought it was more static, but then I realized it was the scratchy sound of hoarse sobbing.

"God. Oh God." It was Andre's voice, harsh and ragged. "Cami," he rasped. "Oh, God, Cami. If you can hear this, come get us. Jesus. Please get us out of here."

Then the receiver went silent.

# Chapter 9

We all stared blankly at one another for a long, silent moment. Then our heads swiveled simultaneously to stare out the front windshield, toward Westlake.

Jeanie was the first to break the spell.

"Dammit!" She scrambled for the long black bag she kept most of her weapons in. The zipper stuck halfway, and Jeanie cursed some more.

"Wait!" I said. "Wait. We need to think."

"We don't have time to wait, Cami. You heard him. Andre's in trouble and it's up to us to get him out of that place." She snarled as she tried to yank the zipper down again.

"Andre's also a trained fighter, Jeanie. If it's as bad as it sounded, what makes you think that going screaming in there is going to make any difference at all? We might get ourselves captured."

"He was crying, Cami." Jeanie's voice was tinged with horror. "Andre doesn't cry."

"So that means it's really bad. I know." I tried to sound calm.

Iverson nodded. "She's right, Jeanie. We need backup." He gestured for Tech One to put a call in to Captain James.

I could taste the metallic tinge of adrenaline in the back of my throat as I waited, trying to find some way to prepare myself to go in. This was going to suck. In an especially creepy vampire way, I suspected.

"Backup's on the way," Tech One announced.

My shoulders slumped in relief.

So, of course, that's when the receiver crackled back to life.

Andre's whispery voice came through the speakers. "Guys. Hey. I don't know if you can hear me. God, I hope you can. We're alone right now. I don't know for how long. This place is full of— They're coming back. Come get us!"

"Full of what? Come on, man, talk to us!" Jeanie leaned in toward the receiver.

"Vampires," Andre whispered hoarsely, as if in answer to Jeanie's question. Jeanie jerked back, eyes wide.

"This is a one-way bug, right?" she asked.

"He must have realized he hadn't finished his sentence," Iverson said.

"I'm not waiting." Jeanie pulled a crossbow out of the weapons bag. "You guys coming with me?"

Wordlessly, Iverson reached out for the bow. Jeanie handed it to him and pulled out a handful of bolts.

I sighed. "I guess this means we're not waiting for Captain James." I reached into the bag and started pulling out stakes, slipping them into all the usual spots: two down each boot, one in each pants pocket, two in each jacket pocket. I wound my shoulder-length dark hair into a knot at the nape of my neck, secured it with a ponytail holder, and slid a Bowie knife into a sheath down the small of my back, the hilt sticking out above my waistband, an additional stake in a special holster right next to it.

I checked my service weapon in my shoulder holster. Guns might not be much good against vampires, but they were great against human servants of those vamps. Then I grabbed one more stake.

"Let's go." Iverson opened the back door of the van and we all piled out.

The night air was beginning to cool around us, with a tiny hint of the slight chill to come later in the season. The full moon shone through the fading blue sky; I hoped we would be able to use its light to find the electronic fence Dr. Richards had mentioned.

The three of us slipped through the trees as silently as we could, slowing as we reached the border between the two properties.

Standing in a line, we stared intently into the oak and pecan trees around us, afraid to take another step in case we set off the alarm. Finally, Iverson waved to get our attention, and then pointed off to the left. I shook my head, and he came up behind me, turning my head and lining my vision up with his pointing finger. There it was.

A tiny red light glinting among the trees. We moved toward it, careful to stay on our side of the invisible line.

We stopped about three feet from the small black box. I scanned the trees around us. Maybe we could go under it. "Cover me," I whispered. I stripped off my jacket and dropped it to the ground, then knelt, preparing to wiggle under the presumed line of the laser.

A strange shiver wiggled through my stomach, sending trails of sensation around and up my back. Goosebumps popped out over my arms, and I glanced behind me, a little surprised to discover no one other than Jeanie and Iverson standing there.

Shaking my head, I turned back to the invisible fence, trying to gauge where the line of the laser might fall.

"I wouldn't do that if I were you, sugar," a voice drawled from above me. With a jerk, I looked up into the trees. There, standing in a Y-branch of the tree, legs crossed at the ankle, hands tucked into his jeans pockets, mostly hidden from below by the leaves, was Reese. He didn't have his hat this time, but he was still wearing his cowboy boots.

As soon as the vampire spoke, Iverson and Jeanie both swung their crossbows up to aim at him. He didn't seem especially bothered by it, but he did take his hands out of his pockets and hold them up in the air.

"Take it easy," he said. "I'm on your side. Ask the lady." That strange thrill went through me again at the sound of his voice.

My squad-mates looked at me out of the corners of their eyes, keeping most of their attention—and their aim—on Reese.

"I don't know." I shrugged. "He might be."

"This is your contact?" asked Jeanie.

I nodded, watching Reese as a slow smile spread across his face, bringing out his dimples.

My stomach flipped as another electric quiver zapped through me.

It couldn't have been because of his smile, no matter how much I wanted to convince myself it had. I had been shaking before I knew he was there.

Iverson took his finger off the trigger, letting his bow point to the sky. Jeanie dropped her aim too, but she still watched Reese narrowly.

"Why are you here?" I asked, injecting steel into my voice and forcing it not to tremble.

"We had a meeting tonight, sweetheart." Reese jumped to the ground. It must have been ten feet down, but he landed lightly, barely bending his knees to take the impact. "You missed it."

"So you followed me here?"

"First I did a little backtracking and found out that Mendoza's group had your partner committed. Then I followed you here." Reaching into the underbrush below the electric fence emitter, he pulled back the leaves of a bush, revealing a second emitter at ground level. "Try to crawl underneath it and this one goes off." He pointed up into the tree. "There's another one about six feet up too."

"So how do we get in?" asked Iverson.

"Up and over is your best bet," Reese said. "That way is left open for vampires." He grinned and his fangs gleamed in the moonlight. I felt, more than saw, Jeanie and Iverson tighten their grips on their bows.

The vampire chuckled—that low unvampy laugh of his—and headed deeper into the trees, paralleling the invisible fence. "Come on. I'll show you the way."

# Chapter 10

Jeanie leveled a serious look at me. "Are you sure we can trust this guy?" she whispered.

"No," I replied. "But right now, I don't know if we can afford not to."

Best not to mention the spine-tingling frisson I felt every time I looked at him.

And every time he stood behind me, whether or not I knew he was there.

Iverson shrugged, shouldered his crossbow, and began following Reese through the trees. I jogged to catch up with them, and Jeanie followed.

"Why are you here?" I whispered when I came up alongside the vampire.

He kept walking. "I was concerned about you."

"No. I mean, how did you know where to find me?" I wasn't entirely sure I wanted to hear the answer.

When he glanced down at me, I felt that tug in my abdomen, like a string pulling me toward him. I stumbled and he reached out to steady my elbow.

"That," he said shortly.

"What the hell?" I rubbed my stomach with one hand.

Raising an eyebrow, he glanced back at Iverson and Jeanie, a reminder of our audience.

Was I seriously considering keeping a vampire's secrets from my own team?

If it meant saving the world, then yes.

*Oh, hell and damn. I am in ten thousand kinds of trouble.*

Reese quit moving and held up his hand for us to stop. "There's our way in. You wait here. I'm going to make sure no one else is using it right now." He moved off through the trees, picking his way through the underbrush.

I could hear our breathing, see the slight mist of it in the warm night air. It took a minute for Reese to return, but every second counted against Andre's life as he fought off vampires.

*Andre is well trained. He's fought vampires before.* Reminding myself didn't help me shake the anxiety.

"All clear," Reese said, pointing up. Between two trees ran a thin wire, about thirty feet off the ground, strung from one tree to another.

This time, my flip-flopping stomach had nothing to do with Reese's presence.

"I'm going to have to walk a tightrope to get in to save Andre?" I said. "No way. I'm not an acrobat. I don't do high wires. You're going to have to find another way in."

"There isn't one," he said. "When we get up there, I'll keep you safe. You'll have to hang from the wire, wrapping your hands and ankles around it, and go hand-over-hand until you get to the other side."

"Like in the 'Be All You Can Be' Army ads." I hoped that the fact that we were still whispering hid the shaking in my voice.

"Exactly like that," Reese agreed. "Ready?" He stepped up into the first Y-branch of the tree, and then reached down to help me follow him. His hand was cool, as usual—no surprise there; he was dead, after all—but as soon as our fingers met, I felt the tugging in my stomach again, pulling me toward him.

The climb up to the wire was easier than I had anticipated. I went up first, and Reese moved gracefully from one branch to another behind me. Iverson and Jeanie followed.

Reese's hands kept me steady, and as long as he was holding on, I found that I wasn't afraid.

I had to keep reminding myself that just because he was keeping me from falling didn't mean I was safe with him.

But it felt safe.

"Here goes," he said. Then he picked me up and held me over the line. *Thank God for his vampire strength,* I thought, then wondered if God was the right person to thank. He let me get my hands and feet positioned, and then swung me around gently so that I was hanging upside down.

I had expected the wire to cut into my hands, but it was coated.
*And if my hands slip, I will fall and die.*
The mere thought gave me sweaty palms.

"Now move," he said. "And don't look down."

It took almost every ounce of courage I had to peel my right hand away from its death-grip on the line and scoot it about six inches farther along, but I managed it. And after that first foot, the going got much easier.

Until I got to the middle and looked down.

My fear of heights isn't rational. It's primal. And my primal instinct, when I let my head fall backwards and saw the ground below me, was to squeeze my eyes shut and hold on to the wire for dear life. I wasn't going anywhere.

Then the wire started swaying and bouncing. I whimpered and held on even more tightly.

"Shh," whispered a voice in my ear. And there was Reese, kneeling down and balancing on the wire above me, in cowboy boots, for chrissakes.

"I won't let you fall," he said. I found myself looking into his eyes. They began shining with a blue light, his pupils widening until they took up all of the irises, then all of the whites. I felt for a moment like I was falling up—up into the blue glow of his eyes. My head spun, then cleared, and my stomach followed suit.

I was no longer afraid.

I nodded at him and unclenched my hands. I moved first one arm, then the other, smoothly, easily. I skimmed the line all the way to the end, watching the ground slide past me as I went.

Reese followed me, stepping across the wire like a cat on a windowsill. The cat we had when I was growing up fell off the windowsill, as often as not. But Reese didn't fall. He didn't falter.

He stepped off the wire and into the crook of two branches above me.

Without thinking about it, I scrambled down to the ground, and Reese followed.

"Okay," he said. "You're good here." I nodded and he moved back onto the wire toward Jeanie and Iverson, stepping along it with that strange motion that most vampires have, all sinuous and balanced.

I realized then that he didn't normally move that way. In fact, until I saw him walk across the wire, I hadn't seen him move in any way that couldn't be described as normal. Human.

I wondered if that meant anything. Were some vamps better able to mimic humans?

*Not human,* I thought.

*Vampire.*

And that's when I started to shake.

I had looked into his eyes and he had taken away all my fear of falling.

I hadn't thought anything of it. Not until he was gone.

And if he could take away that fear, what else could he take away?

I slid down into a crouch and wrapped my arms around my knees. Then, on second thought, I reached behind me and pulled out a stake from its holster at the small of my back.

*If he tries to bewitch me again, I'll kill that S.O.B.*

Seconds later, Iverson swung from the tree and dropped to the ground beside me, Jeanie right behind him.

"You okay?" Iverson asked, frowning.

"I think so." I wasn't shaking any more, but my hands felt ice-cold.

Jeanie followed Iverson out of the tree, and Reese, once again walking the wire, followed her.

"Okay," said Reese, swinging out of the tree to land on the ground. He paused, taking in the stake in my hand and my narrow-eyed glare. Taking one deliberate step back, he nodded at me.

Electricity crackled between us, tugging me closer to him even as I stood up and leaned away from the vampire.

"Let's go." He moved away from the wire and onto a well-worn path.

We emerged from the trees and there, in front of us, lay the back side of the Tudor-style mansion that housed the Westlake clinic.

"Vampires are always expected at night," Reese said. "Stay with me and you'll be fine."

We were halfway across the lawn when the screaming started.

# Chapter 11

The screams came from inside the house, of course.

We all broke into a run. Reese soon outstripped the rest of us, loping across the lawn in a smooth stride that looked wholly unnatural. By the time the rest of us got to the door, he was already out of sight.

We didn't need to see him to follow the screams coming from somewhere above us. We took the stairway to our right—probably originally a servants' staircase, given the narrow, steep steps and the claustrophobic walls.

There was more than one voice, and now that we were closer, I could hear sobbing mixed in with it. And begging. "Please," someone wailed, "not again!"

We tumbled out of the narrow stairway and into a hallway. Iverson and Jeanie were in front of me, so I didn't immediately see what brought them staggering to a halt. I ran straight into Iverson's back. It's a good thing he's as big and solid as he is. If I'd run that hard into anyone smaller, he'd have fallen right into the middle of the mess in front of us. Iverson only tottered a bit before catching his balance.

I grabbed his shirt to keep my own balance, and then edged around him to see what had made them stop.

The lights were off, but moonlight glinted in through several windows. Blood and gore streaked the walls, some of it new and shiny, but most of it dried up, stains of deepest black in the darkness.

Everywhere I looked, vampires were attached to people in various kinds of sleepwear. Some of the humans were trying to fight the vamps off, but they weren't succeeding very well. And worse, some of them weren't fighting at all. In that first glance, I didn't see

Andre or Garrett, but it was hard to tell who anyone was in the semidarkness.

Without hesitation, I reached over to the wall beside me and flicked a switch.

The scene was even worse in full color. The walls were still streaked, but the streaks looked more horrific somehow, ranging from bright, dripping red, to dark black gobs, to a crusty dried brown. The coppery smell of blood tinged the air, overlaid with the more pungent aromas of urine and feces.

The vampires who were feeding looked up, some of them dropping the patients they had been holding, others merely watching us over the bodies of the humans they drained, their mouths continuing to move in time to their victims' slowing heartbeats.

I spotted Reese about three quarters of the way down the hall, pulling a female vamp off a patient and tossing her halfway back toward us.

As suddenly as they had stopped, Iverson and Jeanie moved, both pulling out stakes and wading into what was quickly becoming a more evenly matched fight.

I pulled my own weapons out and moved in the opposite direction, a stake in each hand. There weren't as many vamps down this way, but I knew I needed to watch my team's back. At this end of the hall, four vamps had been busily feeding off their prey, but they were now moving toward me.

I backed up to a blank wall, stake held out in front of me. The vampires were making inhuman hissing noises, staring at me as they inched closer. There were humans on the floor between the vamps and me, and they were stirring now too, clutching their bleeding bits: One clamped his hand to the inside of his elbow, the other to her shoulder, the final to her neck. They looked around blearily, their eyes widening when they caught sight of the vampires.

"Come over to me," I said, motioning them toward me with my head. "I think I can hold them off."

But one of them, the man, actually walked toward the vampires.

"Please," he whispered, "take me."

*Dear God. Defend me from addicts who don't want to be saved.*

At least it distracted the vamps long enough for the two women to scrabble across the hardwood floor and crouch down behind my legs. They clutched each other, their eyes huge in their pale faces.

The man stretched out his arms as if to embrace one of the vampires, a dark-haired male with a Billy Idol-esque sneer on his lip. The vamp brushed the man away with his fingertips, like you might flick away a fly that was bothering you. As far as I could tell, the vamp's fingers barely touched the man, but he went flying across the hallway. He hit the wall with a sickening crunch and slumped down to the floor, unconscious at least, and more likely dead.

The vampires moved toward me, making that spine-unhinging hissing noise and sliding across the floor with inhuman steps.

Without taking my eyes off any of them, I reached into a jacket pocket and removed four stakes. I fanned them out in my hand and held them behind me.

"Take these," I told the two women still cowering behind me. "If they get through me, you'll need them. You should aim for the heart. It's easier than it sounds."

There wasn't time for any more instruction, because all four vampires were heading toward me, eyes glowing blue, tongues flicking across their lips as if in anticipation. I pulled my Bowie knife from its sheath, stepped out from the wall, and crouched slightly, waiting for the lead vamp to telegraph his first move.

I reached down inside myself for the slow calm that always overtook me when I entered a fight. I felt it steal over me, the world narrowing down to this hallway, this moment. Time seemed to slow down, and my eyes narrowed in anticipation.

There it was. The tiniest flick of a motion toward my left, the slightest twitch on the vampire's part, and I lunged that direction, simultaneously ducking, shoving my knife into the vampire's ribs as a distraction, and slamming my stake into his heart.

I hit him dead on, too. I ripped the stake out of the vampire's heart, and a gush of blackened, rotted blood followed it out and across my hand. The knife scraped across bone as I pulled it out, just in time to stake the second vampire of the group. I shoved him as he fell, propelling his body outward toward any oncoming threats. It crumpled onto the ground next to the first kill.

I stepped back again and watched the other two vampires coming down the hall. They crouched slightly, their hands held out like claws in front of them, ready to grab and immobilize me if I gave them a chance.

One of the vampires was a woman with long black hair and extraordinarily pale skin, even paler than the usual run-of-the-mill vampire. She was almost lily-white. The other was also a woman, but this one had color. A lot of color. The kind of color a vampire gets only after she's fed a lot. And recently.

They both circled, trying to get me to move away from the wall, to put my back toward the rest of the hallway—presumably so one of their creepy compadres could ambush me from behind. I lunged out toward them with my weapons, forcing them to back away from me.

There's no telling how long our little corner face-off might have lasted were it not for the rabid snarl that came from behind the vampires. The remaining vamps turned slightly to look behind them. That's when I lunged. And it's also when Reese dove toward us.

I had just enough time to send up a microsecond of a prayer that Reese wasn't attacking me, and then I hit the pale vampire and we went down, rolling on the floor. Her claw-like fingers tangled up in my hair and wherever she twisted, I followed. Her other hand kept going for my eyes.

I waited for the right moment to slam a stake through her free hand, effectively pinning it to the floor. She let out a horrific scream and let go of my hair. I grabbed that wrist and ripped at the remaining strands trapped around her fingers.

Then I ran a stake through her heart.

I looked up to see Reese dropping the other vampire. His mouth and chin were covered in red, and he grinned bloodily at me. I glanced at the vampire at his feet. Her throat had been ripped out— arterial blood had hit the wall in a long spray of droplets. She had a stake sticking out of her chest too.

"Nice work," Reese said. A red drop slid down his chin and I had to swallow rapidly to keep from gagging. The sick feeling in my throat contrasted oddly with the way my stomach pulled me toward Reese.

*Ignore it, Davis.*

I peered down the hall behind him. Iverson and Jeanie were making their way methodically from one end to the other, running stakes through downed vampires and helping shaky patients to their feet.

"Hey," I called out softly. "Any sign of Andre or Garrett?"

"No," Iverson replied. "And we've checked all the rooms down at this end."

I looked around, finally stopping to take stock of the place as something other than a fighting ground.

Most of the heavy wooden doors were open, revealing tiny rooms occupied by a single bed and bedside table. Many of the beds were covered in blood. The wood floors were slick with it too.

"What the hell happened here?" I whispered.

Iverson shrugged. "Feeding frenzy?"

"But you said vampires come here all the time." I looked at Reese, who nodded. "That sounds more like a steady food supply," I continued. "This is a massacre."

"Analyze it later," Jeanie said. "After we find Garrett and Andre."

Right. Priorities.

I eyed several doors at my end of the hall that weren't open. Reese moved up beside me, reached out to the closest closed door, and turned the knob.

I expected a bloody mess. I expected vampires. I expected vampire victims.

What I didn't expect was Dr. Richards, sitting on a bed with her legs crossed, foot swinging, looking intently at her manicured nails, flicking the ashes off a cigarette onto the floor. But that's what I got.

She looked up from her nails and smiled at me.

"Ms. Carlson. How nice to see you again."

# Chapter 12

I stared blankly at her, wondering what the proper protocol was here. How should I reply to that, given that I had spent the last several minutes in this woman's clinic fighting off crazed vampires out for blood?

I finally settled for hello. But I'm not sure it sounded as nonchalant as I had intended it to.

She looked out past me and caught a glimpse of Reese.

"How lovely to see you too, Reese," she said.

He snarled in reply.

Iverson walked up behind me and peered over my shoulder. "Who's this?" he asked me, gesturing into the room.

"That's the clinic director," I said. "Dr. Leah Richards. Want to keep an eye on her while I check the other rooms?"

"Sure." Iverson leaned one arm against the doorframe, while Richards went back to examining her nails and smoking.

I ducked back out of the room under Iverson's arm and motioned for Reese to follow me to the nearest closed door in the hallway.

"So you know her?" I asked as the door swung wide. The room behind it was empty.

"A little," Reese answered.

"Seems like you're on a first-name basis," I said.

"Not by my choice," Reese replied.

I jerked my chin toward another door. "Open that one."

This time, there were two vamps waiting for us. They lunged as soon as the door opened. One of them leapt right into my knife. The other dove into Reese's grip. They were both dead within seconds. I could feel the bond between us tugging, orienting me to his every move, allowing us to fight as a unit.

I tried to ignore it.

"So how did you meet her?" I asked.

"Who?"

I sighed. "Dr. Richards."

"Oh. Her." He reached around me to push another door open. I ducked a charging vampire, and Reese staked it. "I met her the last time I was here." He pushed open the last door, revealing another blood-soaked room. This one was empty of vampires, at least.

I gestured at the carnage. "When you came for…what? A nice hearty dinner?" My stomach turned over—this time not in an electric vampire-connection way—then settled.

Reese moved. "Nope. To detox. I was a patient here once."

"How does a vamp detox?" I asked as we headed back toward Iverson and Jeanie. Jeanie was now helping one sobbing teenage girl stand up.

"A vampire doesn't detox," Reese said. "I wasn't a vampire then. I was a junkie. A human junkie."

I stopped and stared at him in shock. "You were addicted to vampires?"

He raised one eyebrow at me. "It wasn't my original plan, but it…happened. And then I was turned while I was here."

"I don't get it." I gestured at the blood-spattered walls around us. "Why this bloodbath? That's bound to be noticed, and then the clinic will close. Why would any vamp want to shut down an easy source of blood?"

"Let's ask Leah Richards," Reese suggested.

"After we find Garrett and Andre."

Reese opened his mouth to reply, but his words were swept away by the alarm blaring throughout the building. I could hear people on lower floors opening doors. All the lights went on—not only the ones I had turned on earlier, but every single light in the place. I glanced out a window. Outside, floodlights illuminated the entire lawn, all the way back to the woods.

"Sounds like Captain James is here," Jeanie called out to us, yelling to be heard over the alarm.

Iverson waved us on, and then cupped his hands around his mouth to shout. "I'll keep watch up here. Send someone up when you can."

I followed Jeanie down the stairs, and as I rounded the corner out into a hallway, something whizzed past my head, thunking into a vampire who had been standing in the hall. I heard a slight whine, and then the vamp's head exploded.

All over me.

I scooped goo out of my eyes with my free hand and shook it off onto the floor. It landed with an unsettling plop.

Some guy in SWAT gear stood in front of me, an enormous, sleek, black, dangerous-looking gun in his hand—a Colt M177. I'd heard we had new anti-vamp ammo for those. I hadn't realized it exploded.

Two more SWAT team members were on their way up the stairs, turning to make room for Jeanie as she passed them. They were wearing black and carrying Colt M177s.

"I like the new rounds." I pulled my badge out of my pocket and flashed it. "Detective Cami Davis. I need your help. Come with me. You clear the lower floor?"

"Yes, ma'am," the shorter of the two said. "Nothing down there but civilians. No hostiles."

I looked at the two officers closely. The taller had light blond hair shorn close to the scalp and watery blue eyes in a long, narrow face. The other one was maybe five feet seven, dark hair and blue eyes, muscular and attractive. Neither of them could be more than twenty or so.

Glad they were willing to play backup as I searched for Andre and Garrett.

"I'm looking for a couple of undercover cops," I said. "You guys know Andre Perricone?"

They looked at each other, and then the shorter one answered. "I recall being introduced to him, ma'am."

"What about Quentin Garrett?" I wasn't hopeful, since Garrett had been undercover for a while. I wasn't surprised when the two officers shook their heads.

"Okay, then. You two had better watch my back while I search."

"Yes, ma'am." They both contrived to look even more serious and alert than they already did.

"What are your names?" I asked.

"I'm Savage," the shorter one answered. "This is Bier."

We moved down the hallway, peering into rooms as we passed them. In most of the rooms, patients sat quietly on their beds, eyes wide as they peered back at us.

"All of you stay in your rooms," I instructed in my loudest I'm-in-charge voice. "If you stay in your rooms until someone comes to get you, you won't get hurt." I realized as I said it that it might sound like a threat of some sort. Like a bank robber who tells his hostages they won't get hurt if they cooperate. That wasn't the image I was trying to convey, so I added, "We're here to help you. Please stay in your room until I come back." That was better. A little.

At the end of the hall, I pushed another door open and walked into a scene even worse than the one upstairs.

There was blood everywhere. It ran in red trickles down the walls and dripped onto the floor. Whole gobbets of bloody flesh stuck to the floor—and to the ceiling, I realized, as an unidentifiable piece of someone fell to the floor in front of me with a sickening splat.

My head spun. This was the hall I had left Andre in earlier that afternoon. "Oh, God, no," I whispered aloud.

There were several bodies on the floor, mutilated almost beyond recognition.

"You two," I said, pointing at my SWAT guys, "check to see if any of these people are still alive. And get those other two guards out there in here." They both stared at me with shell-shocked eyes. "Now!" I barked as I started ripping open doors.

Both officers jumped as if they'd been hit with a cattle prod, and Bier started feeling for pulses.

The rooms were almost as bad as the hallway, gore dripping from unexpected places. The third door I opened revealed two naked male bodies lying spread-eagle on the bed in a widening pool of blood, their torsos ripped open from their necks to their crotches. I had to breathe in deeply several times to keep from vomiting before I could move around to the head of the bed and look at their faces.

Their eyes stared glassily at the ceiling. Neither was one of my guys.

The next two rooms revealed more bodies, more gore. I was almost becoming inured to the sight of so much carnage. I was even noticing the horrific smell less and less. But it was a brittle sort of acceptance, one I knew would crack if I found either Garrett or Andre dead, smeared in his own blood.

I was about to open a third door when one of the SWAT officers called out to me. "I think we've found something," he said.

"What is it?" I asked.

"This door is blocked from the inside," he told me, indicating one of the middle doors.

I hardly breathed. I wasn't sure, but I thought it might be the room Andre had been unpacking in earlier in the day. I pushed the officer gently out of my way and turned the knob. Locked.

"Get a battering ram," I told the officer who had called me over.

I knocked on the door several times while I waited, but no one answered.

It took five or six solid kicks for the hinges to give way. At first glance, the room seemed empty. Bloodstained sheets covered the bed, but no one was in sight. I moved in warily. The window was still covered with bars, so whoever had locked the door had to still be in the room. No closets. That left only one place.

Holding my gun out in front of me, I carefully squatted down and peered under the bed.

"Oh, thank God." I closed my eyes and blew out a breath in relief.

Andre's eyes, alive and aware, stared at me from under the bed.

# Chapter 13

Andre lay on his stomach, a bloody stake in one hand. His other arm was wrapped around someone under there with him.

"Cami?" His voice was much smaller than I remembered it.

"It's me," I said soothingly. "Come on out." I turned my head. "Go see if EMS is here," I instructed the SWAT officers who had knocked in the door in for me. "As soon as you find them, send a paramedic down here immediately." I peered under the bed again. "And tell them Garrett is unconscious."

I extended my hand toward Andre, who took it as he crawled out from under the bed. I handed him off to an officer and reached back down to get a grip on Garrett. One of the other SWAT officers knelt down to help, but I waved him away.

Then my stomach flipped, sending electric sparks out through my body, and I knew Reese was behind me.

I let him help.

We pulled Garrett toward us, grabbing first his shoulder and then gripping him under the arms. His head flopped loosely back and forth, and my breath caught in my throat as he slid out from under the bed.

I hadn't realized how thin he'd gotten.

His legs poked out from the bottom of his plaid boxer shorts like two pale sticks. He looked pitiful, like a sick old man. I felt tears gather in the corner of my eyes. I blinked furiously to keep them from spilling over. "I'm so sorry," I whispered. "I'm so very, very sorry."

I set him down on the floor, grabbing a blood-spattered pillow from the bed and turning it over so Garrett's head could rest on the clean side.

I was still holding Garrett's hand when a paramedic, followed by the officer I'd sent to find him, showed up. The paramedic began checking Garrett's pulse and breathing.

"Has he been out since you found him?" he asked.

"Yes. He hasn't even moved at all," I said.

He nodded. "Okay. It looks like he's in shock. Let's get him out to the ambulance."

"You"—I pointed at the remaining SWAT officer—"go make sure the rest of the building is clear of vamps. Remember: Shoot as soon as you see the whites of their fangs. Unless it's this guy." I gestured toward Reese, who nodded seriously.

The rest of the EMT team came rolling in past the officer as he left the room.

"Are there many survivors?" I asked, though I was afraid the question might send at least one of them over the edge into permanent shock—one EMT's face was already a clammy white.

Her partner answered me. "Not of the ones who were attacked—most of them are dead, and we've stabilized the ones who didn't die. But there seem to be a lot of patients who didn't get attacked. We've called in social services. Those people are going to need serious help."

And I knew whose fault that was.

I turned to Reese. "I think it's time for us to ask Dr. Richards exactly what was going on here."

* * *

Back upstairs, I motioned Iverson away from Richards's doorway. "Andre and Garrett are downstairs. Not seriously hurt. We're going to see what we can find out from the director."

"You and the vamp?" He cut his eyes toward Reese, and then glanced away when the vampire returned the look.

I nodded. "I'll be okay. Check on Jeanie? I haven't seen her in a while."

As Iverson headed down the stairs, Reese leaned against the doorjamb of Richards's room and stared in at her. "Want me to do this?" he asked, narrowing his eyes and lifting one corner of his mouth, just enough for the overhead light to glint off a fang.

*Good cop, bad cop? I'm in.*

I sighed. "Okay. But you can't kill her. Not until I've had a chance to talk to her."

"Okay. I won't kill her." He licked his lips.

"Don't maim her either, Reese. I mean it."

He finally looked at me. "No killing, no maiming. Got it."

"I'll be back in a minute." I took a half step toward the stairs.

Richards sat quietly through all of this, until Reese started to move into her room. Then she scrambled across the bed and shrank back into the farthest corner. "You can't come in here," she said. "This is my room, and you are not invited. Not invited!" The last bit rose to a shriek as Reese covered most of the room in one stride and loomed over her, placing his hands down on the mattress on either side of her.

"No, Leah," he said, looking into her eyes as she shrank away from him. "You gave all vampires an open invitation when you started your nightly party here. You can't take it away now."

"Not all vampires. Anyway, you can't hurt me." Richards's voice was more shaky than certain, but she sat up a little straighter as she spoke. "The Sanguinary promised to protect me."

Bingo.

Tilting his head so that his cheek brushed against her hair as he leaned in, Reese whispered, "The Sanguinary isn't here, Leah."

She whimpered. "Please don't bite me."

I stepped into the room and leaned one shoulder against the wall, crossing my arms. Richards's eyes flickered toward me, and then back to Reese.

"Look at me, not her," the vampire said. "She can't help you."

I shrugged.

"They'll kill me if I talk," she whispered.

"I'll kill you if you don't." Reese's grin was filled with an unholy delight as he leaned in and sniffed her neck.

Richards let out a little moan. "It's blood magic."

Reese pulled back a little. "How does that work?"

"Every time a vampire takes blood, it draws power too. Magic. You feel it, don't you? When you take blood, you feel the power it can give you."

If I hadn't been watching so closely, I might not have seen Reese's split second of complete stillness. He might not have known about the blood magic beforehand, but he knew exactly what the clinic director was talking about. He recovered quickly, though.

"And tonight?" He gestured toward the doorway. "Why the massacre?"

"To open some kind of door." Her voice dropped. "They needed more power. Every time, with every one, they've needed more power," she whispered.

My stomach dropped in sudden dread. "Every one what?" I spoke up for the first time.

Richards glanced at me. "Every ceremony. Every sacrifice."

"You mean the dead women, right?" I took a step toward her, my hands fisting at my sides as I fought the urge to shake the information out of her. "The Sanguinary is sacrificing them?"

She nodded, eyes wide. "They are planning something really big, and tonight's the lead-in."

Tonight's butchery was only the lead-in? What the hell was the Sanguinary planning?

"Where?" Reese demanded, grabbing her upper arm. "Where is tonight's sacrifice?"

"I don't know. I swear, I don't know."

I believed her.

But that meant that somewhere in the city tonight, a woman was dying—was being tortured to death by vampires—and I probably wouldn't be able to find her in time to stop it. Helplessness swept over me, leaving me shaking and weak.

"But we interrupted it, right?" I asked. "They didn't get the power they needed."

Richards watched me, her eyes calculating. "Maybe not. But still more than they've had before."

"What's the big plan? What is tonight leading up to?" I stepped up to loom over her threateningly, momentarily forgetting my role as good cop as I edged Reese out of my way.

She shrank away from me. "All I know is that it's set for Halloween."

A brief, startled noise from Reese suggested that he might know what she meant, but I pushed the clinic director anyway. "And you probably don't know where that's happening either, right?"

The clinic director smirked at me, regaining a bit of her confidence as she flouted her superior knowledge. "Maybe I could find out."

"How?" Though he had stepped out of my way, Reese still hadn't let go of Richards's arm.

"I have a phone number."

My first instinct was to say, *Not a chance in hell*. But in the end, that's what this was: a tiny chance to save one woman from hell.

And maybe save the entire world.

I nodded at Reese. He let go of her arm and stepped back.

But when we brought her a phone—tapped and monitored—and she dialed, no one answered.

I counted each ring like the tolling of a bell on an old-fashioned clock, counting down the moments until someone else died.

A death knell.

Though we didn't get an answer, the other phone was turned on, so Tech One and Tech Two were able to give us a general area to search—somewhere within a few miles of downtown—but even diverting all available units didn't give us access to every home, every building, every basement, every attic.

We had Richards call over and over, for hours on end, until eventually the number began going straight to voicemail, an automated message only.

I pulled Reese aside after the last failed call. "Richards is a problem. We can keep all the other humans on lockdown and under guard while we sort out which ones knew what they were getting into, and which ones were dupes."

"But Richards now knows you're a cop, and she is also connected to the admin." He pursed his lips for a brief moment, and then nodded decisively. "I'll take care of it. I can make sure she doesn't remember you."

I shuddered. The thought of a vampire digging around inside my mind sent chills up and down my back.

As my vampire partner left to muck up Richards's memory, I tried to distract myself by helping with the clinic cleanup. It took us all—detectives, SWAT, uniforms, EMTs, and CSU, everyone who wasn't out crawling the streets looking for the Sanguinary and their horrific sacrifice—the rest of the night to get the clinic cleared out and the patients transferred to real hospitals. I didn't envy the doctors and morticians that night. Then again, we all had serious work to do.

Somewhere in the controlled chaos that is an active crime scene, Dr. Leah Richards disappeared.

I bawled out the uniform watching the room where we had stashed the clinic director, threatening to write him up for his incompetence.

It wasn't until later that I realized Reese was gone too, probably in connection with his plan to wipe the doctor's mind. I didn't want to be part of that, but I did want to talk to Reese in private about his sudden appearance at Westlake, about the strange connecting tug I'd felt between us—that pull I could still feel, if I concentrated on it. It was a twinge that I knew I could follow. It would tell me where to go to find Reese. When I realized he was no longer at the clinic, I closed my eyes, feeling a magnetic draw, pulling me almost directly south.

Downtown. Near the phone Richards was calling. Near the sacrifice?

I considered joining him—but then the call came in.

Another body.

The latest sacrifice victim.

# Chapter 14

This victim's body was at the Cathedral Shrine of Our Lady of Guadalupe, only a few blocks away from the Winspear Opera House.

The crime scenes were getting closer to one another.

This was the first time a body had been found inside a building—the first time we'd found the primary crime scene rather than a body dump. There hadn't been time for a dump—the killer had been interrupted by the priest coming in to prepare for morning mass and had fled the scene.

"Think they chose the spot because it's a church?" Iverson asked as we stepped out of his unmarked car and headed into the cathedral. Jeanie had stayed behind to oversee the wrap-up at the clinic scene.

*Too many vampire crime scenes tonight.*

The redbrick exterior of the cathedral gave way to cool white walls sweeping up into darkness. The reflected glow of streetlamps shone through the rose window above the nave, the light washed away before it reached the floor by the additional lamps the crime-scene techs were shining on the body draped across the altar.

I paused for a moment to look up the long aisle, flanked by pews. This cathedral had one of the biggest congregations in the country—second only to St. Patrick's in New York City—and the room was huge.

Did these murders have a religious significance? Did vampires care about religion at all?

We knew crosses didn't work on them. Stakes to the heart, beheading, sunlight. They were otherwise invulnerable.

Though the lack of any older vamps suggested that they might not actually be immortal.

I shrugged. "For all we know, they could have been doing all of the sacrifices here."

The crime-scene tech—Bradley, the same one who had pulled the scrap of paper from Felicia Monroe's hair—straightened up from where he had been peering at this dead woman's out-flung arm.

"Doubtful," he said, continuing his perusal of the victim. "If all the kills had happened here, the perp would probably have known the priest's schedule. And there would probably be more bloodstains on the altar. I can't say for sure until the labs come back, but I think we're looking at just one murder in this location."

He turned to face us. "But you'll probably want to see this." As he moved around to the other side of the altar, he pointed at a wound on the victim's dangling hand, blocked from our view until we moved up the steps onto the parquet floor.

A bright blue light flashed from her palm. The tech pointed at it with his pen, careful not to cross the beam or allow it to touch him. Then he traced the beam to its endpoint at the back wall, where instead of creating a small circle, the light seemed to expand until it created an oval about two feet tall and a foot wide.

"It was bigger when we got here," the tech said. "And watch this." He pulled a penny out of his pocket, hefted it in his hand, and then tossed it toward the oval.

It should have bounced off the wall.

Instead, the coin hit the light, where it slowed and seemed to hang for a moment, as if moving through some viscous fluid.

And then it was gone.

"What the fuck?" Iverson breathed.

The tech shrugged. "Hell if I know. But nothing we've put through has come back."

"Has anyone touched it?" I asked.

"No. Earlier, I tried to mark the wall—trace a circle around it— and my pen got pulled out of my hand. Once that happened, I didn't let anyone else close to it."

"Does it go both ways?" Iverson asked, peering at as closely as he could without risking touching it.

Bradley shrugged. "Nothing's come through yet."

"Okay," I said, trying to maintain my composure. "Tell us what else you've got."

As the tech circled the victim, pointing out the various wounds—the ones I had come to expect, lately, given their repetition across the victims—I considered the possibility that the crackpots were right: Vampires came from somewhere else.

Maybe from somewhere that could be reached through that blue light, that strange little portal that continued to shrink, even as I watched it out of the corner of my eye.

So the Sanguinary vamps were using these portals to…what? Bring through more vampires for a war against humans?

I rubbed a hand across my grainy eyes, working to put it all together.

Feeding on blood gave vampires a kind of power, one connected to blood magic.

That blood magic could be strengthened through a massacre like the one at the clinic tonight.

And that stronger blood magic could be channeled through a sacrifice like the one tonight, opening the door for more vampires? So why the serial sacrifices? What was the end-goal of the Sanguinary?

"Thirteen's a powerful number." Reese's voice was quiet behind me, and it was all I could do not to jump.

"What do you mean?" I didn't even bother to ask what he was doing here—or where he had gone when he left the clinic.

The tech had moved away to another part of the cathedral, and Iverson had followed him—I had been too caught up in my thoughts to notice—so we were all alone for a moment.

"This is body number twelve, right? The twelfth sacrifice?"

"Unless you count the clinic. There were a lot more than twelve bodies there."

Reese shook his head. "That wasn't a sacrifice. These are careful, controlled. That was a massacre." Reese followed the line of blue light to the spot on the wall, now shrunk to just a few inches across. As he stepped closer, the light pulsed. "You know the history of vampires, right? The public one?" he finally asked.

"Sure," I said. "You guys have always been here, but vamps were a minority—until there were enough vampires to survive a potential war, they all stayed in hiding."

"I don't think it's true," he said.

When he didn't speak for a long moment, I finished the thought for him. "You think the crackpots are right—the ones who tell their stories to the *American Enquirer* and post their crazy theories on the Internet. Vampires didn't come from this world."

Reese nodded, watching me carefully.

"So where did they come from?" I tried to keep my voice level.

*Leave it to me to get hooked up with the one vampire who bought in to the craziest bullshit out there.*

Then again, the pulsing blue oval on the wall—a hole in the world leading nowhere—suggested that maybe Reese wasn't so crazy, after all.

"I know it sounds insane," he said. "But fifteen years ago, so did the idea of vampires. I think there have been a few vampires here for a long time. They came from wherever, found a world full of walking, talking meals, and stuck around, turning a few other people here and there. But there weren't many of them. About eleven years ago, there was a series of ritualistic murders exactly like the ones you've been investigating, but in New York City."

I shook my head. "No way. It would've popped on one of the databases when we entered these in the system."

"Hear me out. Not long after, vampires started showing up in huge numbers—first in New York, then in other places all over the world. And in all those places, there were murders like these. Exact same MO."

"How do you know that?" I asked.

He paused for a long moment. "Because I was the lead detective on a case like this one in Denver. And suddenly, all the cases disappeared from the databases. Then the cops who were working on them started disappearing too."

"You're a cop?" My rising voice echoed in the empty sanctuary, and I looked around to see if anyone else had heard, but Iverson and Bradley were just moving out the front entrance.

He grinned. "Was a cop. Now I'm a vampire."

"Okay. Let me get this straight. You were a cop, then a vamp junkie, then a vampire?"

"Didn't plan on either of the last two," he said dryly. "The Denver Sanguinary got me addicted, drove me back home to Texas, checked me into Westlake. I've spent the last eight years showing the Dallas Admin that I've converted completely." He paused, then added quietly, "And figuring out what the fuck they're doing here—and why they need to kill people to do it. I may be dead, but I'm still a cop at heart."

"Do you have proof of all this?" I asked.

"Some. Not as much as I'd like." He shrugged. "But in the end, it doesn't matter. If I'm right—and I'm sure I am—then the murders are actually acting as some sort of focus to bring vampires through from wherever they originate. Stopping the murders in one place isn't enough. We need to find out how to close down their ability to create portals altogether."

"How does all of this tie in to the Sanguinary and the blood house?" I asked.

"The number thirteen has power in this world. The Sanguinary has arranged for thirteen blood sacrifices to create the portals. As far as I can tell, almost all of the vampires in the admin are part of the Sanguinary group. That means that most of the vamps in charge are also involved in opening the portals. I need to get in with them, to get more information." Reese's voice sounded determined.

"How did you even know there are portals?" I glanced at the shrinking blue oval. "Before today."

"Hints, whispers. Nothing certain." He shook his head and his jaw tightened. "But someone in the Sanguinary knows more, and I'm going to find out."

"So you think the massacre at the clinic was used to power this sacrifice?"

Reese nodded. "Richards said this was a lead-in to something bigger. And like I said, there's power in the number thirteen." He held his hands out toward the portal, like someone warming them at a fire. "And power in the number in other worlds too, I think. I can feel something strong calling to me."

"What will happen with sacrifice thirteen?" I asked.

"I don't know, exactly." He shook his head as if brushing away the pull of the blue light and turned to face me again. "But we can't let it happen—we can't let the Sanguinary gain that much power."

As he spoke, the portal flared for a moment, the outline of a hand pushing through from the other side. I gasped and pointed as a penny—maybe the same one Bradley had sent through earlier—bounced out and across the floor.

As if that had used the last of the portal's energy, the light collapsed with a faint pop, then winked out.

I stared at the blank spot on the wall for a long moment before I turned to Reese. "I can't believe I'm about to say this, but I think you're right."

He caught my gaze with his, and his pupils began to swirl with a light that matched the portal's glow. My chest squeezed, as if my heart were reaching out to his, the energy connecting us drawing us closer and closer to one another. He dropped his voice to a whisper. "And I think I know when they're going to kill their next victim. I know how we can stop the Sanguinary."

*　*　*

Two hours later, Reese, Iverson, Captain James, Chief Paige, and I sat around a conference table at the station, the door to the meeting room closed and locked. I had smuggled Reese in through a back entrance, and we had spent the last few minutes outlining our plan.

"Are you positive?" Chief Wallace Paige asked.

"As sure as we can be, sir," Iverson responded.

"Magic," Captain James said, shaking his head. He blew out a sigh. "You're certain the next sacrifice is set for Mendoza's party?"

Reese nodded. "It's the biggest vampire gathering I've ever heard of. Every local member of the Sanguinary will be there. We can take them all out and keep them from bringing through whatever is on the other side of that portal."

"And taking down the vamps won't add to this magical power?" Chief Paige was focused, his deep voice rumbling and intent.

"We can't know for certain." Reese opened his palm in a one-handed shrug. "But if vampire deaths opened the portal, I don't think the Sanguinary would have hesitated to sacrifice their own."

"This is why you sent me in, sir," I said. "To find out what Sanguinary was. Now that we know the connection between the Sanguinary and the killings, we can stop them."

Everyone around the table nodded.

"Very well." Paige leaned back in his chair, nodding. "You two see if you can get an in to this party without drawing any additional attention. We'll get ready on our end."

Reese smiled, but it was a grim expression. "Halloween night—seems like a perfect time to kill vampires."

# Chapter 15

I caught a ride back to my apartment with one of the uniforms.

I had spent the entire night at horrific crime scenes, and the thought of sleep—of allowing myself the luxury of unconsciousness in a world where women were tied down to altars so their bodies could be sliced into the right shape for vampire magic to flow through them—made me dizzy and sick. So instead, I went for a run. The early morning haze had burned off quickly, and the bright sunlight beat down on my face. Usually I hate the Texas sun, the way it pounds on my head. We native Texans know to stay out of the midday heat.

Today, though, I welcomed the sun—particularly its value as a vampire repellant. The thought of the night before left me shivering, even in the middle of the daylight.

I didn't want to remember what I'd seen at the clinic, at the church, so I increased the pace, adding extra miles to my usual route.

It was later than usual when I got back home, nearing ten o'clock. I had finished my bottle of water before the extra miles, and was panting when I began my slow-down walk to my door. Inside, I climbed into the shower. The hot water sluiced over me, and I watched as little eddies swirled down the drain. When I closed my eyes, the swirling turned to blood, flowing across every other image in my mind. The people I loved, the ones I worked with, everyone I knew or saw. All covered in blood.

Fifty years—that's how long we'd have until the vamps were in charge, until the whole world looked like that charnel house of a clinic. Until every house was a blood house, and bodies covered in strange, carved markings littered the street.

I shuddered, leaning my forehead against the cool tile in front of me and letting the water pound against my back.

Stopping the Sanguinary was the answer to keeping the world from sliding under.

Reese held the key to stopping the Sanguinary.

We were going to take them down.

My eyes felt hot and dry by the time I toppled into my bed. They weren't much better when I woke up after dark, but a glass of water helped. A quick trip to the nearest fast food restaurant—a Whataburger—did wonders for my mood, if not my diet, and by the time I got back home, I was feeling almost alive again.

I dialed Garrett as I ate and listened to the phone ring on the other side until his voicemail answered. I called Iverson, and he said the EMTs had taken Garrett to the hospital, but he had checked out earlier in the day.

I didn't leave a message on Garrett's cell.

I did, however, leave a message on Reese's phone, asking him to call me. He didn't.

By the next evening, I felt good enough to go for another run, pleased to finally be getting back into my training routine. I gave it an extra push, adding the same few miles to the end of my usual circuit—enough so that it was almost dark by the time I got back home.

I had just put my key into the lock on my own door when Reese appeared from the shadows of the entryway to the apartment next door.

I nearly screamed aloud before I realized who it was.

I knew I should probably be panicking over the fact that he had found where I lived. I wasn't listed in the phone book. My address didn't show up online—I knew, because I had Googled it. But Reese's appearance wasn't entirely unexpected, given that strange connection between us. At the thought, my stomach flip-flopped. I focused on the black garment bag he carried slung over his shoulder.

I sighed, images of the clinic threatening my memory. "What do you want?"

"Another trip to the blood house."

I groaned.

"You're not up for adventure and romance?" He emphasized the first syllable of *romance*. Then he smiled, and my heart twisted. I wasn't sure if it was because of the connection, or just because he was beautiful.

Ignoring the thought, I rolled my eyes. "Not really."

His expression grew serious. "Mendoza put the word out that he's got some big announcement to make tonight. I'm concerned that the events at Westlake Clinic might have prompted whatever he's got planned tonight."

"Okay." I nodded, suddenly as grave as he was. "Give me ten minutes and I'll meet you downstairs."

"What are you wearing?"

"I don't know." I eyed him warily.

"Try this." He handed the garment bag to me.

"Oh. Thanks," I said.

"Maybe you should wait to see if it fits before you thank me," he said.

I stared at him, my hand running absently across the garment bag. "Have you seen Garrett since Westlake?" I asked.

He responded with only the tiniest shake of his head.

I sighed. "I'll be right back."

I knew it was a bad idea to accept gifts from a vampire. Even a beautiful vampire. Even a beautiful cowboy vampire who seemed like he might be one of the good guys.

But he'd brought me a dress.

And vampires have such good taste. They may be bloodsucking fiends from hell, but they're generally stylish hell-fiends.

This particular hell-fiend was no exception. The outfit was stunning. It wasn't even really a dress. It was more of a suit. The top was a rich black satin jacket with silver-and-rhinestone buttons and a plunging neckline. The bottom was a pair of black satin pants overlaid with flowing black chiffon. It was perfect evening wear for someone who might have to kick vampire ass at some point during the festivities.

He'd thought of everything. Including loops inside the jacket's décolletage that were perfect for holding a stake in place. And a pair of low-heeled sandals with straps that wrapped around my ankle and calf and also served to hold stakes. And finally, he'd included earrings and a necklace—either high-end zirconium or diamond. I suspected diamond.

After a quick shower, I put the outfit on. It fit perfectly. I twirled my hair into a French twist and pulled some tendrils down around my face to soften it, then dusted my face with powder, smudged on some eyeliner, and added lipstick. There. Now I looked like I belonged in a blood house.

I rummaged through my closet until I found my one black evening bag and moved the essentials—lipstick, powder, cell phone, cash, stakes—over to it.

When I walked out of the apartment, Reese was waiting. "You look lovely," he said.

"Clothes by Reese," I said in my best advertisement voice. "Now can I say thanks?"

He grinned. "Sure."

We walked down the stairs to the parking lot, where Reese ushered me into a big black Ford dually pickup. And despite the fact that I was with a vampire—even though I knew it was foolish—I felt completely and utterly safe. Knowing that the only vampire I had to worry about at the moment was Reese felt strangely freeing.

Halfway down the road past the complex's gate, he glanced in the rearview mirror. "Don't turn around. Someone is following us."

I fought the urge to peer over my shoulder. "Are you sure?"

"Positive. And he's been behind us since we left your place."

"Crap. It's probably the FBI," I said.

Reese took that more calmly than I anticipated, simply raising an eyebrow. "Is it you they don't trust, or me?"

"After my conversation with the agent the other day? Probably both."

He nodded, and without warning, spun the truck down a side street. The car tailing us missed the turn, and Reese killed the headlights before making several more turns. I craned my neck around to look out the back windshield. When I saw headlights, I spun around and sank down into the seat, but they turned off on another road. Not our followers.

Reese settled back in the seat. "I think we lost them."

I wasn't sure how I felt about being followed by the Feds, and that worried me. I was afraid I might be losing track of which side was which. Or at least, which people—and vamps—were on whichever side was mine.

Another thought struck me. Why hadn't Agent Chandler—or any FBI agents, for that matter—shown up at Westlake, or the cathedral?

Was Chandler acting on his own?

I pushed the idea aside. As long as I didn't get pulled into any interdepartmental shenanigans, I was happy.

We parked half a block away from the blood house. As we made our way down the street, Reese pulled me into the shadowy entrance to another building.

"Hey," I said warningly. "No biting, remember? We don't want you sending any extra power to the Sanguinary by feeding on me."

"We still need to have the smell of fresh blood on you," he said, "or you're never going to pass as my Claimed bloodgiver."

He reached up with one hand and pushed the satin covering my shoulder over to the side to reveal my bite scars. His own marks were still fresh, but the cuts didn't hurt—not like the wounds I had gotten when fighting vamps.

I had removed the bandages from those bites for this outing, and Reese ran his fingers lightly over the two small scabs. His touch made me shiver, but I told myself it was only the night air.

The other vamp's bite wounds, on the other side of my neck, were still raw. I had left them covered.

"So how are we going to manage this?" I whispered. I licked my lips nervously, then wished I hadn't when I saw how Reese watched my tongue. Like a predator. My heart beat faster.

Reese caught his breath but maintained that uncanny eye contact. "You have to quit doing that," he said, his tone raw. His hand clamped down on my shoulder, just under the bite marks, and I winced.

"Doing what?" My own voice was feathery, almost nonexistent.

"Being afraid of me." His nostrils flared in an especially vampirey way.

I took a deep breath to calm myself.

Reese closed his eyes and carefully unpeeled his hand from its grip on my shoulder. He, too, took several deep breaths.

"I'm sorry," he finally said in his normal voice. "I'm not entirely sure what happened just now."

"You thought about eating me." The panic I'd been feeling seconds earlier worked its way out as a higher pitch.

His eyes narrowed thoughtfully. "I did consider it."

"Oh, fuck. This isn't going to work." I started to push my way past him and back onto the street.

He grabbed my arm. "I can't do this without you. And I can control myself," he said, his voice turning wry, "as I think I just proved."

I eyed him warily. "Can we make me smell like blood without you going all creepy vampire guy on me?"

He laughed, and this time it was a normal laugh. "Yes."

"Okay. I guess."

"I think, though, that perhaps I ought to change my original plan."

"Which was?"

"Never mind." He fished around in his pocket and came out with what looked like an ice pick.

"What's that?" I asked.

"It's an awl."

"An awl? You carry an awl around in your pocket?"

"Before I was a cop—back in college—I used to be an artist. A sculptor. I keep this with me"—he looked at it—"as a reminder. Also for protection. No one expects a vampire to use a weapon other than his teeth."

"I promise you," I said, "no one fighting you would be looking for an awl even if they didn't know you were a vampire. No one ever expects an awl." I paused. "What's wrong with a gun? You were a cop after you were an artist. No one expects a vamp with a gun, either."

He laughed, but didn't answer the question. Maybe he had a gun too.

"This is going to hurt, isn't it?" I asked.

"Probably."

I stood very straight, squared my shoulders, and titled my head to the side to give him better access. "Okay. Go ahead."

He stepped close to me and with two swift jabbing motions used the awl to open first one puncture mark and then the other.

"Ow," I said. My shoulder throbbed.

"Here." Reese licked his thumb and ran it gently across the wounds. The throb dulled and my shoulder tingled, and I focused on that, rather than the sensation of his skin whispering across mine.

I wiggled the shoulder experimentally. "This is great. I think I've found the next breakthrough in anesthesia. Vampire spit."

"We'll be rich," Reese said dryly.

"Do I smell enough like blood?" I asked.

Reese sniffed the air. This time his nostrils stayed nice and unflared, unvampirey. "Yes. But I need to mix my scent with it a bit more, I think." He licked his thumb again.

"I take it back," I said. "This has got to be unhygienic."

Reese slid his thumb over the wounds again, then wiped the blood off the spit-covered thumb and onto his coat. "There," he said, sniffing the air again, "that's better."

"So can we go now?"

Reese nodded, and I slipped out of the doorway.

I didn't know how much longer I could stand going back and forth between trusting him and fearing him.

But here I was, going into a blood house with him, smelling like blood, without other backup.

In the end, trust won out, aided by the thrill that ran through me and to him, drawing us ever closer together.

Even without an exchange of blood.

I closed my eyes for a second and took another deep breath. Then I followed Reese in.

# Chapter 16

The blood house was packed. Apparently, every vampire who was any vampire and his bloodgiver had come out for Mendoza's big announcement. Looking around, I was glad for the outfit Reese had bought me. Dressing down would have been the best way to stand out in this crowd tonight—and the last thing I wanted to do was stand out in the midst of a bunch of vampires.

Make that a bunch of glittering vampires.

Most of them were draped in diamonds. This group probably comprised the biggest chunk of all the vampire power in Dallas. If I'd known about it in advance, I could have arranged to wipe out most of the bloodsuckers here.

But how? Bomb the place? That would kill all the bloodgivers too. Did I really want to kill all the humans along with the vampires?

Did I want to kill Garrett? Because there he was walking toward me with cute-vampire Dahlia hanging off his arm. He was dressed in a tuxedo and looking perfectly handsome.

Until I looked into his eyes.

*Handsome and haunted*, I amended silently.

"Well, hello, Reese," Dahlia said in her little-girl voice. "I didn't know you'd be here tonight. You're usually not interested in these sorts of things."

"What sorts of things?" he asked.

"Transfers of power, of course," she said. "Right, Garrett, sweetie?"

Garrett hadn't taken his eyes off me while Dahlia had been talking. "Right," he muttered absently. "Can I talk to you for a minute, Cami?"

"I guess." My shrug wasn't as casual as I had planned.

Garrett peeled Dahlia off his arm and grabbed me by the elbow, practically dragging me toward one of the unoccupied, curtained rooms. We stopped before we got there, though. His grip was weaker than it had ever been before.

"What are you doing here?" Garrett hissed.

"Me?" I pulled my elbow out of his hand sharply. "I'm not the one with the vampire problem, just out of the clinic from hell. I'm undercover, remember? After Westlake, you should still be in the hospital. What are you doing here?"

He ignored my questions. "Everyone's talking about Reese's new Claimed one. I assume they mean you?"

"So what?" I asked.

He grabbed me by the upper arms and shoved his face into mine. "So I want to know where you get off telling me not to let the vampires touch me when you're playing Claimed girl to Reese."

"Let go of me, Garrett." I shrugged and pushed his hands off my arms. "Not that it's any of your business," I hissed, "but I am *playing* Claimed. He doesn't get to drink my blood."

"Bullshit," Garrett said, snarling. "Mendoza says it's true—you really are Claimed."

"Mendoza says it? What are you doing talking to Mendoza?"

He didn't even have the grace to look abashed. "He owns the place."

"And you're in here often enough to talk to him." I put my hands on my hips. "Well, clearly, everything he says must be the God's honest truth. Oh, wait. He's a vampire. Maybe he's not telling the truth. They lie, Garrett." We were leaned in close to each other now, practically spitting our words into each other's faces.

"Yeah? Then maybe you ought to think about whether or not your friend Reese is lying to you."

"You know what? This is none of your business. But it is mine. My business, Garrett. My job. You know, what I do for a living? What you're supposed to do for yours too. And if you screw it up because of some weird vampire-bloodgiver jealousy, I swear, I'll—"

"What? What will you do, Cami?"

Suddenly I felt deflated. "This conversation is over, Garrett. What I do is my business. And what you do is yours. You want to ruin your life by letting some leech drain it away, that's your problem. Just don't blow my cover, okay?"

I didn't even wait for an answer. I turned around and left. I didn't have the time or the patience to discuss this with him any longer. I had a job to do, and I couldn't let Garrett interrupt it. That was my new mantra: *Not my problem.* I repeated it to myself over and over as I headed back toward Reese, who had taken a seat at the bar.

"Trouble?" Reese asked as I sat down next to him.

"Nothing I couldn't handle," I said.

Out of the corner of my eye, I saw a woman slide into the seat next to me. Her dark curly hair flared out in a perfect wedge from the crown of her head to her shoulders, falling artfully across one eye—that cool look women with lots of curls can sometimes manage. I'd always envied that particular look.

"Vodka," the woman said in a throaty voice. "With." Her hair swooping across her cheek hid her face from me, but the voice sounded familiar.

She reached into her bag and pulled out a cigarette, then fished around for a light. The bartender handed her drink to her and flourished a flaming Zippo.

"Thanks," she said, and leaned in to light her cigarette.

That was when I recognized her.

Leah Richards.

I elbowed Reese. He turned to look at me, and then did a classic double take when he saw who was sitting next to me.

*Holy shit. She's a vampire.*

She wore a black sheath dress that fell to the floor, skimming across her curves. When she moved, the dress shimmered with deep red undertones. Her skin, always pale, was now porcelain white. Her eyes had been rimmed with black and her lipstick matched the burgundy in her dress.

She must have felt us staring, because she turned to meet my gaze.

"Yes? Do I know you?" She took a long drag off her cigarette and blew a stream of smoke at me.

I fought the urge to cough and wave my hand in front of my face. Instead, I shook my head and reached for a stake.

Richards's gaze flickered over to Reese. "How lovely to see you again." She had said almost the exact same words at the clinic. Had he wiped her memory of him being there too?

"When were you turned?" Reese asked. He moved around to stand between Richards and me.

*Is he protecting her?*

Richards stared at him, then off into the middle distance for a moment. "I'm not sure," she said, shaking her head and taking another drag off her cigarette. "I woke up in a hospital and knew I had changed."

"Have you talked to Mendoza?" Reese asked her.

Her stare sharpened. "Why should I?"

"No reason. I thought you knew him. He owns this place, you know."

"Yes," she said softly, almost to herself. "I know that."

I fingered the stake I had tucked into my waistband.

If I moved quickly enough, I could stake her. God knows she deserved it.

But that wasn't why we were here.

As I was debating killing the former clinic director, Dahlia slid up next to Richards.

"Look, Leah, I found someone for us to play with." She turned around and tugged on her hand, speaking to the person behind her. "Come on."

And, of course, Garrett moved out from behind her.

I couldn't stand to watch him with them. Instead, I turned to face Leah and Dahlia. "It's been lovely seeing you all. I've had a very nice time." I grabbed Reese's arm. "We're going somewhere else now." I marched away, Reese's sleeve bunched in my fist. He turned back to wave at the little group by the bar, his arm pulling out behind him as I kept walking.

*I've had a very nice time.* I always say that at the most inappropriate times. I shook my head.

Reese let me get him halfway across the room before stopping me. "If we want to take out the Sanguinary all at once, we have to get into that ball. And if Mendoza is hosting it, we won't get in without an invitation. So we need to figure out how to get one. Tonight. Politicking won't work; we're out of time. We have to draw attention to ourselves."

I sighed. He was right, of course. I stared around the blood house, hoping for inspiration. What would be sure to get us invited to the Sanguinary's Halloween ball?

The chandelier in the center of the room cast a hard, glittering light over the space, sparkling off the jewels worn by the women. Its illumination didn't reach the far corners, though; those were lit by softly glowing lamps on the tables in the balcony. Many of the bleeding rooms had their burgundy velvet curtains drawn to conceal what was going on inside them, though the gasps and moans from them were audible. On the main floor, the edges of the room stayed dark, the few still-open bleeding rooms shadowy and indistinct.

A dais had been raised in the middle of the room. A woman in a black sequined gown stood upon it, singing some sort of vampire torch song with a smoky voice and the suppressed quiver of energy that I had come to recognize as peculiarly vampiresque.

In fact, the whole room virtually hummed with that vamp energy.

Vamp energy.

Fueled by blood.

Reese and I shared energy, even when he wasn't taking my blood.

And just like that, I knew the answer.

Blood.

# Chapter 17

If I didn't do it now, I wouldn't be able to do it at all. I took a deep breath, turned to Reese, and said, "Let's go to a bleeding room."

Reese nodded with a disconcerting lack of surprise. "Yeah," he said. "That'll be a good place to talk."

Oh, hell. He didn't get it. I was going to have to be more explicit. But not yet.

He reached out and took my hand. We worked our way through the room, moving toward the sides. Most of the bleeding rooms were still occupied. We finally found an open one toward the front. As I stepped inside and sat down on the velvet couch, my heart started beating faster.

Reese stopped, one hand on the curtain as he prepared to draw it closed. "We could go somewhere else, you know." His brow creased in a slight frown as he looked at me.

"No." My voice sounded breathless. I shook my head. "This is good."

"Okay," Reese said. "If you're sure."

"I'm sure."

"I'm not going to hurt you, you know." Reese's frown deepened.

"I know," I squeaked.

"Then what's wrong with you?"

"Nothing." My shoulder tingled where he'd bit before, neither painful nor soothing, but somewhere in between. The sensation of being alive. And knowing it, I couldn't help wanting more.

"Look, let's leave." He pushed the curtain all the way open.

"No." There. My voice sounded steadier. I looked at him and caught a movement out of the corner of my eye. Looking out into the main room, I saw Garrett standing stock-still and staring at me.

"Close the curtain," I said quietly and firmly.

"Okay." Reese shrugged and drew the curtain closed, cutting off Garrett's stare.

I settled farther back onto the couch, and then shuddered, a little from excitement, a little from fear.

"What is wrong with you?" he asked. "You're acting strange."

"Strange? How strange? I mean, strange how?"

He shook his head. "Look. I don't know what your problem is, but you've got to get hold of yourself. We need to figure out how we're going to get into this party." He lowered his voice and leaned toward me. "If we're going to take these guys out, we need to come up with a plan."

"You're going to bite me," I whispered. My voice trembled more than I would have wanted it to, but at least I'd managed to say it out loud.

My invitation to him.

For the case, I told myself.

Reese threw himself back onto the couch with an exasperated explosion of breath. "Dammit, Cami. Just because we're in a bleeding room doesn't mean I'm going to bite you. Calm down."

"No," I said. "That's the plan. You. Bite me. Now."

Reese stilled. "Why?"

I pulled the collar of my satin top wide, exposing the scars on my neck and shoulder. "For power. They already think I'm Claimed by you. Bite me. Take whatever power you're supposed to get from it, pass it along to them."

Reese sat back in the far corner of the couch. "I don't know how to take power."

"This connection between us—you feel it, too, right?" At his silent nod, I continued. "Is it normal?"

"No," he said quietly. "It's like nothing I've ever heard of before."

"Then tap into it, pass it on to the Sanguinary. Let's see if we can use it to get their attention."

His pale face was as stone still as it was stone cold. "You're sure you want me to?"

My voice dropped, almost to a whisper. "I'm sure it's necessary, Reese. We need to have at least one thing in our favor."

"We've got your Sucker Squad," he said, in something approximating his usual tone.

I smiled. "Yeah. And we'll get them to come in on Halloween. But we won't be able to do even that if we can't find out where the ball is. We need an invitation, and to get that, we need to try this."

"Okay." Reese took a deep breath and scooted closer to me on the couch. I pulled the satin even farther away from my neck. He leaned in and I turned my head away from him, squinching my eyes closed.

Reese hesitated over me and then leaned back. "I can't do it if you're going to look like that."

*Dear God, please give me the patience to deal with reluctant vampires.*

Though come to think of it, I wasn't sure God would listen to a vampire killer praying for enough patience to convince a vampire to bite her.

"Reese," I said gently, "I'm terrified. But this is important." I took a deep breath and schooled my face to an impartial expression.

"Okay." He nodded, and once again, I pulled the neckline of my jacket back. He leaned forward, burying his face in my neck.

So of course I got the wild giggles.

"What?" he demanded.

"Nothing," I gasped out between guffaws. I cleared my throat and got control of myself. "Nothing. Go ahead."

He leaned in again and sank his teeth into my neck, right where it met the line of my shoulder. I felt them slide in with a sharp pain, like a pair of needles, and suddenly I didn't want to laugh anymore.

I felt his fangs pumping out whatever drug it is that vampires use to calm their victims—whatever it is that creates bite addicts. It moved like liquid heat across my shoulder, down my arm, into my fingertips. I felt it slide through my veins and into my heart, which began throbbing in time to the motions of Reese's mouth on my shoulder.

I whimpered a little, but when I felt Reese's fangs start to glide out of my skin, I pushed his head back down.

The heat from his mouth pooled in my gut and slid down the veins in my legs, leaving a sexual ache behind. I moaned aloud and closed my eyes. My breath started coming faster and faster.

But something was wrong. Even through the fog of fang-induced pleasure, I knew this wasn't working the way it was supposed to. I wasn't feeling any sort of overwhelming power moving from me to Reese.

For that matter, despite the heat of the moment, I wasn't feeling any of that spine-tingling connection between us, either.

"Wait," I said. "Stop." I hit Reese on the shoulder. "Stop it!"

He unlocked his jaw and raised his head, his eyes wide. "What?"

"You're not doing it right. Whatever it is you're supposed to do to get power from me, you're not doing it."

He wiped his hand across his mouth, and then moved my jacket back onto my shoulder. "I guess it isn't going to work." He turned from me and started to stand up.

"Wait a minute." I grabbed his hand and pulled him back down onto the couch. "You did this on purpose," I said. "You didn't even try to draw power from me. Dammit, Reese. Do it again. You get down here and you bite me good." I pointed at my neck. "I want you to take blood and power. Right now."

He laughed a little at my tone. "Okay. But I'm worried about what this will do to you."

"Don't be," I said. "We can handle this."

We leaned toward each other and he once again slid his fangs into my neck.

This time, the heat from his fangs became a fire, rushing through me and igniting every nerve ending into tingling awareness. The brush of his lips, the gentle caress of his tongue against my skin made me writhe with pleasure. His hands trapped me on the couch, pushing me back into its softness. I strained upwards, pushing my neck against his mouth.

His lips never quit working against my throat, but he picked me up, cupping my butt in one hand and using it to pull me farther down on the couch while his other hand cradled the back of my head. Leaning over me, he gently pressed one knee against my thighs until I opened them. He knelt with one leg on the couch and the other standing on the floor, both arms still holding me. Lifting his head, he looked searchingly into my eyes. A shudder ran through me, lust and power combined.

"Are you sure you want this?" he asked. His voice was raw and ragged. His eyes were almost completely dilated; I could see only the tiniest rim of white around the edges of his pupils. They were beginning to glow with that strange blue light.

"Yes." I whispered. "Please."

He leaned in and kissed me. His mouth was cool and I could taste the tinge of copper that was my blood on his tongue. A single thought raced across my mind—*this should be really disgusting*—and was gone. It wasn't disgusting at all. It made the fire in my veins burn hotter and brighter, and I tugged at Reese's jacket, pushing it off his shoulders and down his arms. His kiss deepened and I moaned in the back of my throat.

I managed to undo his bow tie with one tug, and then we were both lying on the couch, my legs wrapped around him, his tongue deep in my mouth. I played with his fangs with my tongue, testing their sharpness. He bit down, ever so slightly, and his fang slid inside my tongue. My breath caught in my chest, but the sharp pinpoint of pain faded as a small amount of blood welled to the surface. Reese melted against me and whimpered as I ran my tongue against his, mingling the taste of him with the taste of blood.

He traced a trail of kisses down my neck and into the cleavage line of my jacket, then licked one long line back up to the puncture marks on my shoulder. I pushed my head back against the couch and drew in a shaky breath. With one hand, he unbuttoned my shirt and slid it gently off, pushing my bra out of the way as he moved down to kiss my breasts. My nipples grew taut under his tongue, and I whimpered with pleasure.

I fumbled with his shirt and pants, finally pushing them to the floor. He moved his mouth down to my stomach, smiling against it as I used my feet to finish pulling his clothes off of him.

He gently slid one fang through the top of my bellybutton as if piercing it for a ring. I nearly screamed aloud with the combined pain and pleasure, barely managing to capture the sound in my throat. Moving back up across my body, Reese covered my lips with his own, and I whimpered into his mouth.

Reese lifted up just enough to use both hands to slide my pants to floor. I stared into his deep blue, glowing eyes.

With one smooth motion, he bit my neck and slid into me at the same time.

And the world exploded around me.

It was light and motion and electricity, blinding and paralyzing me even as I wrapped myself tighter around Reese. The liquid heat inside me pooled in my very center, gathering and swirling as we moved against one another, building to a crescendo as we strained to match thrust for thrust.

Tiny flames of pleasure licked across my body as my sweat slicked across Reese's chest and my blood gave his skin a rosy, heated glow. I could feel something powerful twist and surge around me as we moved in perfect harmony with one another, until it erupted around us and through us, moving across our skin and through our veins, pushing us over the edge to release. We clutched each other, crying out.

And then we lay together in silence.

Reese rested his forehead against mine, eyes closed, and I blew out a shaky breath. "Wow," I said quietly.

"That's an understatement." Reese's eyes were green again, his pupils having shrunk back down to something approximating their normal size.

"So," I said. "How do you feel?"

He grinned that cocky grin of his at me.

"No." I pushed his shoulder in mock anger. "Not that. You know. The power stuff."

"Oh. That." He unwrapped his arms from around me and leaned back. "I don't know." He frowned and shook his head.

"You don't know? Shouldn't you?"

"I don't know, Cami. That was like nothing I've ever experienced before." He laughed a short, breathy laugh and sat up, reaching down to pull on his pants.

"Oh." My voice was quiet. I, too, grabbed my clothes and began struggling back into them, suddenly aware that there was nothing but a velvet curtain between me and a big room full of overdressed vampires and their buddies.

As I pulled on my jacket and began buttoning it, I noticed several tiny puncture marks all along the tops of my breasts. I stopped briefly to examine them. I hadn't even noticed when Reese had bitten me there.

Reese, having finished buttoning his own shirt, touched me under the chin until I looked into his eyes.

"Hey," he said quietly. "Whether it worked or not, it was worth it."

"I certainly hope so." I found myself taking a big breath and suddenly having to blink rapidly to avoid crying.

"It was," he said.

I simply nodded and finished dressing.

"Ready to face your public?" he asked.

I reached up and wiped a smear of lipstick from his mouth. "I am now." Squaring my shoulders, I turned to face the entrance as Reese pulled the curtain back. I froze, looking out into the room.

And into the faces of what seemed like a hundred vampires, all of them standing, silent and still, in a semicircle about six feet away from our bleeding room.

All of them staring back at us.

We definitely had their attention.

# Chapter 18

"I think maybe it worked," I whispered out of the side of my mouth to Reese.

He didn't answer.

The big ring of vampires continued to stare at us.

In retrospect, we should have perhaps realized that the perfect silence we had experienced inside the bleeding room was not metaphysical in any way—it was echoed by the silence outside the bleeding room. We should have been able to hear the din of conversation, glasses clinking, feet shuffling, bloodgivers giving blood, and the like. But we hadn't. Because all of that had stopped so that everyone could come gape at us.

"Do something," I whispered. Don't ask why—it wasn't like the vampires surrounding us couldn't hear me. But I felt a strong need to at least pretend that they weren't following every syllable of any exchange between Reese and me.

"Like what?" Reese didn't bother to keep his voice down.

"I don't know. Say something."

Reese cleared his throat.

He was saved from having to make some awkward speech, though. A rustle in the until-then perfectly still crowd caught our attention. The vampires parted, and Mendoza made his way through, followed by another vampire. This vampire was young looking— he'd probably been turned when he was eighteen or nineteen—with dark hair and a slight build. He wasn't any taller than I was. He was attractive, but not astonishingly so, unlike many of the vampires in the room. The woman following him was thin and pale and wan, either a haggard-looking mid-twenties or a slightly rough mid-forties. I was guessing the former.

"Who are they?" I whispered to Reese.

"Lane Boyd and his Claimed. He's Mendoza's second-in-command."

The group stopped in front of us, closer than the rest of the vampires but still maintaining a slight distance.

Mendoza nodded to each of us. "Reese. Cami. You made quite a stir here tonight."

Reese didn't bat an eye. "Sorry if we disturbed you," he drawled.

"Not at all, not at all. The performance was quite...interesting."

*Performance?*

I was going to curl up and die right there.

"Well, thank you." Reese grinned and spared a glance for me.

Boyd's eyes narrowed. "And this is your usual experience?"

"I like to think it's different every time." Reese put his arm around my waist and pulled me close. "Every time is...special."

"I see." Boyd turned his back on us and muttered something to Mendoza, then walked away. The crowd melted before him. His bloodgiver trailed along behind, looking for all the world like a lost puppy.

Mendoza smiled and rubbed his hands together. Neither of those things made me feel especially safe. He was far too predatory for my comfort. "If you'll excuse me?" he said with a smile. "I have an announcement to make, and then I would like to speak with you again."

"Of course." Reese smiled back.

Mendoza turned to the crowd of vampires and announced, "If you please, I would like to invite everyone to join me in a celebratory drink."

I didn't like the sound of that. I didn't want to celebrate anything. I wanted to go home and try to figure out what had happened to me. For one thing, it's not like me to have sex in a semipublic place. Much less with a vampire.

Between Reese's possessive stance and Mendoza's celebratory attitude, I was beginning to wonder if this had been choreographed, maybe as part of Reese's plan to make his way into the Sanguinary.

How much of our power swap back there had really been my idea?

Or had Reese and Mendoza manipulated me into doing what they had planned all along?

The sick feeling in the pit of my stomach suggested that I might not want to examine the answers to those questions too closely.

The vampire crowd slowly dispersed—with many glances back at us. When the majority of them had turned their backs on us, I clutched Reese's elbow and whispered in his ear, "Get our invitation to the ball so I can get out of here." As an afterthought, I added, "Please."

"We really do need to stay for Mendoza's announcement." Reese led me slowly toward the bar, and the vampires in our path melted out of our way as if by magic.

"What just happened?" I hissed.

"I'm not entirely sure," Reese said.

"Do you feel any different?" I asked.

"Not really. Do you?"

"No. But those vamps in there sure were acting like you were the Second Coming."

He laughed out loud. "I think most of them would be a lot more dismayed by the Second Coming."

"Okay," I said. "But you know what I mean."

His brow furrowed, the smile fading from his face. "Yeah, I do. We need to try to figure this out."

"We need someplace private."

He looked at me speculatively. "Would you feel comfortable going back to my place?"

I raised my eyebrows at him. "After what happened in there? I don't think going to your place is going to bother me."

He nodded. "After Mendoza's announcement."

Before we got to the bar, though, a scuffle at the front entrance caught my attention.

*Not my problem.* I started to look away, but the crowd between me and the door cleared for a moment and I got a look at who was involved in the disturbance.

It was Chandler, the FBI agent who'd shown up at my door two days ago.

*Oh, hell. I guess we didn't really lose that tail, after all.*

He could blow my cover with a single word, and all this would have been for nothing.

This issue was my problem after all.

I spun around to Reese. "Check out what's happening in the entryway," I said.

He craned his neck to see above the crowd. "Damn," he said.

"My thoughts exactly. Shall we go?"

But Reese was already ahead of me. As he brushed past Mendoza, he murmured, "I'll deal with this." He got to the entrance first, and by the time I caught up with him, he was already talking.

"No, he's with me," Reese was saying. "Agent, I believe you were trying to see me?"

Chandler stood with his back against a wall, one hand holding out a badge, the other reaching into his jacket, probably for a stake. I made a negating motion down by my waist, hoping the agent would see the flick of my wrist and interpret it correctly. His eyes flickered from Reese to me, and he slowly withdrew his hand, flashing the palm long enough for everyone to see that it was empty.

"Yes," he said slowly. "Yes, I was."

"Good, then." Reese turned to the two vampires who were guarding the door. "We'll step outside and speak to the agent, okay?" They narrowed their eyes at him, but finally nodded.

With a whoosh of air, I let out the breath I hadn't even realized I'd been holding.

We moved through the foyer. No one spoke until we were outside.

"What was that?" Chandler demanded.

"A private party," Reese said smoothly.

"What kind of party?"

"A casual get-together among friends."

"Sure it is." Chandler eyed our formal wear suspiciously. "What does this blood house have to do with the Sanguinary?"

Reese led us out the front entrance and onto the sidewalk, countering Chandler's question with one of his own. "Why were you following us tonight?" he asked.

Chandler didn't bother to deny the accusation. "I have a few more questions for Ms. Davis."

Reese shook his head. "I don't think so."

"Excuse me?" Chandler started to puff up, but then he looked into Reese's eyes.

We're trained not to do that—to look at cheeks or noses, never eyes—but I knew from first-hand experience how easy it was to forget that training.

Reese used Chandler's brief moment of inattention to catch the agent's gaze with his own. "You'll forget all about following us tonight," the vampire said. "You will go straight home. You'll forget about this address, this building. You spent tonight waiting for Cami Davis outside her apartment, but she never left the complex. You finally gave up and went home to get some sleep."

I glanced from Reese to Chandler. Chandler's mouth had gone slack and he nodded as he continued to watch Reese's eyes.

I shook my head and put my hand on Reese's arm to stop him. He spared a glance at me, and then continued speaking. "You'll wake feeling happy and refreshed, and forget you ever heard of the Sanguinary. Now go."

Chandler turned around and moved down the block. He looked like a sleepwalker, or maybe a drunk staggering home.

I hoped no other agents saw him like that.

"Why did you do that?" I demanded.

"I had to," Reese said. "He knew too much."

"You could have done something else. Lied, maybe? Made up some cool story? You didn't have to muck around in his memory. That's horrible."

Reese stared deeply into my eyes. "Cami, I think maybe you should forget this too."

I stared directly into his eyes and enunciated clearly as I spoke. "Fuck you, Reese. I will not forget it."

Reese blinked, and an expression like surprise crossed his face. Then his eyes narrowed speculatively. "Really? You aren't going to forget it?"

"No. I won't. And I want you to quit trying to make me. You can't make me do anything." I turned my back on him. "God. Men suck. Especially vampire men. And vampire-addict men. All of you."

I heard Reese chuckle deeply behind me. I shook my head. "I'm going back to hear Mendoza's announcement, and then I'm going home. You can do whatever you want."

With that, I stalked inside.

Of course, my dramatic exit was somewhat foiled by the fact that Reese caught up with me in the foyer.

"Look," he said. "I'm sorry. If it bothers you that much, I won't do it again."

"Yeah? Which part? Hypnotizing other people? Or trying to hypnotize me?"

He grinned. "Both. Either. I won't do either of those things again."

"Really?" I stared at him suspiciously.

"Really. I swear."

I sighed. Who knew how much a vampire's promise might be worth? As I'd said to Garrett earlier, they lied. But it was better than nothing. "Fine," I said. "I accept your promise. And your apology. Don't do it again. Ever."

"Okay, darlin'. I won't." His drawl was back. That made me more nervous than anything else that had happened all evening.

# Chapter 19

We weren't even halfway across the room when I saw Mendoza headed our direction.

"I'm so glad you returned. I was worried you would miss my speech later. And after you'd had such an exciting evening already."

I felt a blush crawl across my cheeks. Mendoza turned his eyes toward me, taking in my flushed cheeks, then glanced back at Reese. "Oh, how charming. I do love it when they show their blood like that. Quite the aphrodisiac, don't you think?"

It was all I could do not to pull out my stake and do him in right then and there. Reese must have felt me twitch, though, because he put his arm around my waist and pulled me in close.

"Remember, Mendoza," he said quietly. "My Claim, my blood. Admiration is one thing. Desire is another."

With the words *my Claim, my blood,* the connection between us intensified. The room twirled as a wave of hot nausea passed over me. My head spun and my knees went weak. If Reese hadn't been holding on to me so tightly, I think I might have fallen down. I swallowed hard and blinked my eyes rapidly, desperately trying to maintain my equilibrium.

I felt a tremor run through Reese's hand, but Mendoza didn't seem to notice.

The administrator's voice dropped to match Reese's. "Are you threatening me?"

"Consider it a warning."

They locked eyes for a moment; then Mendoza broke contact. "Very well. I don't believe I could trust a man who didn't protect his Claims. My apologies." He took my hand and brushed his lips across it. They were ice cold. It was all I could do not to snatch my hand back and wipe it off.

I nodded, not trusting myself to speak. Not that I would have known what to say, anyway. I felt a bit like a piece of meat with two dogs growling over it. And with a sick feeling in my stomach, I realized that with vampires—even Reese, possibly—that was very close to what I was. Lunch and a good lay, all in one.

That thought made me truly ill. I looked up at Reese tentatively, hoping that snarling look would be gone from his eyes. It wasn't. I had to get away from him for a minute. I pulled myself out of his grip—*death grip*, I thought, and then shook my head to dispel the image. "I need a drink. Will you go get me one?"

"Sure," Reese said in his usual drawl. He grinned down at me. He was beautiful. But he was also every bit as dead as Mendoza. "Want to come with me?" he asked.

"No. I'll wait over there by the wall." I indicated a space between two open bleeding rooms.

Reese frowned a little. "Okay. I'll be right back."

I made my way to the spot I had indicated, hyperaware of not touching anyone I passed.

The touch of cold, dead, animated flesh might make me vomit.

I leaned back against the wall, savoring the touch of the cool wall against my overheated back. There was something terribly wrong with me—I felt feverish and sick.

Reese returned and handed me my drink, something clear and fizzy. I sipped it gratefully. Sprite. Without the special blood house additive. Without alcohol, as well.

"Are you okay?" Reese asked me. "You felt that, too, right?"

I nodded. "I'm a little hot," I said. *Not that you'd understand that anymore*, I added silently.

He frowned and started to say something, but then stopped.

I took another sip of my drink. I was beginning to feel better— the strange wave of nausea was receding. In fact, I realized, I was feeling better than I'd felt in days. "Remind me why we can't kill them now?"

"We want to get all the Sanguinary. They might not all be here tonight, but they'll all be at the Halloween ball."

"Right. Kill 'em all. Not just some of them." I looked out across the room and saw Dahlia heading toward us determinedly, Garrett firmly in tow.

Hurriedly, I gulped the rest of my drink and handed the empty glass to Reese. "Go get me another drink, would you?"

He followed my gaze. "You sure you're up to it?"

"Go get the drink. I'll deal with these two," I said.

With a shrug and a grin, Reese complied.

I leaned back against the wall and waited.

"Cami, darling," Dahlia sang out as she approached, making kissy noises at me. "I'm ever so glad to see that you and Reese are still doing well. I was afraid you might be tired after your performance."

Garrett didn't say anything. He had dark, bruise-colored shadows under his eyes and his face was thin and pale.

*Looks like Garrett's been giving blood too.*

He couldn't afford to lose any more.

"You know," I said, turning to Dahlia, "you really shouldn't abuse your...what is he? Bloodgiver? Anyway, you shouldn't mistreat him like that. They'll last longer if you're kind to them."

Even that didn't get a rise out of Garrett. I would have preferred a repeat of his anger from earlier in the evening. I hated seeing him like this, hated the thought of him turning into a shadow of himself.

"But you see," said Dahlia, in that sweet, little-girl's voice of hers, "I don't care how long they last. I care that they're all mine while I have them." She turned around and caressed Garrett's cheek. He stared at her blankly. "And this one, you see, is all mine."

My nostrils flared and I fought the desire to pull out a stake.

*I'm going to kill this bitch if Reese doesn't get back soon.*

With a flash of heat that seemed to burn across my face and leave a sick taste in my mouth, I felt him. Reese, to my left, headed my way. As if seeing double, I could see the crowd parting in front of him, see them bowing toward him—me?—see their faces looking into his eyes even as I saw their backs facing me.

"Oh," I whimpered, and slumped against the wall, fighting to maintain my balance.

"Garrett, darling, your old partner can't bear to see you with another woman," Dahlia said. "Were you in love with him, Cami?"

I held a hand over my eyes and tried squeezing them shut. Instantly, the double vision cleared. When I opened my eyes again, I was looking at Reese handing me a glass of juice. I reached out and took it, gulping the cold liquid gratefully.

"I felt that," he murmured. "Are you okay?"

I shook my head, and then shrugged. I didn't know if I was okay or not.

"Your pet and I were discussing old loves," Dahlia said. "Now what was her name again—the one you had before this one?"

"I can't imagine what you're talking about, Dahlia," Reese said. "If you'll excuse us, please." He put one hand on the small of my back and held my elbow with the other, supporting me as I stepped away from the wall.

"Oh, but you can't go," Dahlia said, grabbing my forearm with both hands. Her voice hardened. "I've barely gotten started."

I lifted my head and stared at her. My vision blurred for a moment, then cleared. "Don't touch me," I growled, and snapped my arm out in a motion meant to merely dislodge her, to shake her off me.

Like the vampire in Westlake had flicked the addict away and sent him sailing.

And just like the addict at Westlake, Dahlia lifted into the air and flew across the room, landing ass-first on a small, decorative table holding a lamp against the far wall and crashing into the mirror above the table.

As if I had tossed her with vampire-level strength.

*What have we done?*

The shards of mirror showed half a roomful of stunned humans staring back and forth between Dahlia and me. A glance at the room showed the rest of its non-reflective inhabitants, also staring open-mouthed at me.

"Are you sure you want to stay for the announcement?" I muttered to Reese.

He didn't reply. I turned around to look for him and discovered him standing right behind me, mouth hanging open, just like rest of the vamps.

# Chapter 20

The blood house stood completely silent. Not that it was ever a loud place, particularly, but there was usually a sort of general hum—of conversation, of moans and muffled screams from the bleeding rooms, of crystal glasses (with and without blood) clinking. But now there was nothing but the shuffling sound of people shifting surreptitiously from one foot to another as they tried to stand still, and the sound of Dahlia pulling herself off the table. I could hear the tinkle of glass as her movement sent mirror shards to the floor.

Looking up, I realized that Mendoza was standing on the dais in the middle of the room.

"Ah," he said, raising his glass toward Reese and me. "That was quite an introduction. Thank you. Now I may begin."

All through the room, heads turned to watch him, and then back at us.

My eyes grew huge, and Mendoza's smile grew wider. Taking a drink from his wineglass, he drew a deep breath and prepared to speak.

"As many of you know," he began, his voice carrying easily across the entire space even without the apparent aid of a microphone, "events last summer left us with, shall we say, an opening in our administration. We lost one of our administrators when he was arrested and subsequently executed." His eyes drifted across the room, then landed squarely on me.

I had arrested that vampire.

He was the one who had left all the scars on my shoulder.

I fought an urge to look around wildly, to see if Mendoza was actually looking at me or at someone else. And then I fought the urge to run like hell.

*He knows,* I thought frantically. *He knows I'm a cop.*

The only thing that kept me from fleeing the room was Reese's hand gently touching my back, right between the shoulder blades. It was a calming touch, a touch that sent power and strength flowing through me.

*Garrett,* I suddenly thought. Garrett told Mendoza. I knew it as surely as I knew anything.

But then Mendoza's gaze moved past me, and I was no longer certain.

Besides, if my cover was blown, if Mendoza knew I was a cop, we would have to scrap the operation. And I wasn't willing to do that on a hunch.

"We, therefore," continued Mendoza, "have an administrative opening." A murmur swept through the crowd and Mendoza held up his hand, waiting for quiet. "The administration has met and rearranged our upper levels. I have resigned my post as Dallas administrator and will be accepting the position of North Texas administrator."

He paused for a moment, looking around the room, apparently making eye contact with specific people, though I couldn't tell which ones.

"We will be looking for someone to take over the position of Dallas administrator." Again the crowd murmured; again Mendoza held up his hand until they were quiet. "I will announce my replacement at the ball; it seems appropriate, somehow," he said, smiling. "We will, of course, be looking for someone of special power, special abilities." His eyes scanned the crowd again, but this time I could tell exactly which vampire they landed on.

Reese.

I turned my head to look at him, but Reese stared back at Mendoza with an inscrutable gaze.

*Mendoza is considering making Reese the head of the Dallas vampires?*

We had hoped for an in to the Sanguinary. This was much more. My first instinct was that it was bad. I felt my shoulders tense.

Reese must have felt my reaction, felt my muscles preparing for flight, maybe even felt my panic through the bond between us, because he moved his hand from my back and slipped his arm around my waist. I stiffened, and he held on tighter.

"Don't do it," he said, leaning down to whisper in my ear. "We'll talk about it when we get out of here."

Mendoza continued speaking. "We will be accepting nominations and applications until tomorrow, October 30. I look forward to seeing you all at my soiree. In the meantime, please enjoy yourself tonight." He stepped down from the dais and made his way through the crowd, pausing to chat with small groups of vampires who stopped him, presumably those who wished to congratulate him on his step up in the administration.

I pulled on Reese's arm.

"In the administration, Cami," he whispered. "It's where we want to be."

I wasn't sure which part scared me more: that I was in a room full of vampires who might turn on me at any moment, that Mendoza might see me as a threat, or that Reese might actually be interested in the power Mendoza seemed to be offering him.

I stuck to Reese's side. It seemed the least of all the evils in the room at the moment. I took several deep breaths to calm myself.

Once my panic had subsided, I noticed that Reese's own breath had caught in his throat at some point when I was trying to calm myself. He was only now taking in a couple of shaky breaths, and I was reminded of his earlier reaction to my fear.

My fear provoked Reese's desire. Add that to the list of things that terrified me.

The next thing I noticed was the way the other vampires were treating Reese. It wasn't anything overt. But before, the other vampires in the blood house had ignored him, too intent on their own pleasure or power to pay a relative nobody any attention. Now, however, they acknowledged him. They weren't quite deferential— after all, he hadn't actually been named as Mendoza's successor— but they made eye contact as they passed. They nodded to him. A few of them quietly spoke, mostly in greeting, when they would have ignored him before.

And Reese handled it smoothly.

As if he'd been waiting for this.

The fear in the back of my mind threatened to surge forward again, and I had to consciously beat it back down. Reese glanced at me out of the corner of his eye and frowned.

"Are you okay?" he whispered, leaning in close.

"Fine," I said. "Ready to get this over with, that's all."

He nodded, but he didn't quit frowning.

Finally, after what seemed like an eternity, Mendoza made his way around to us. I took a deep breath when I saw him approaching.

Reese spared a brief glance for me and rested his hand across the middle of my back. Once again I felt his support—not really as a physical sensation, but as a sort of strengthening of my resolve, as if his hand on my back were actually helping me find my balance.

I consciously let the feeling wash over me, deciding to accept it for now and examine it later. After we'd dealt with the immediate situation.

"Good evening." Mendoza said, nodding to each of us. "I have something for you." He reached into his pocket. I flinched, certain for a moment that he was going to draw a gun. Then I realized how stupid that was. Vampires don't shoot people. They rip them to shreds with their teeth.

He pulled an envelope out and handed it to Reese. "I hope you'll both join us," he said before strolling back into the crowd.

I felt my entire body sag and realized that Reese had removed his hand from my back. The envelope was nowhere to be seen, tucked into Reese's own pocket.

"Let's get out of here," he suggested.

"It's about time."

Not until we were halfway to the exit did I allow myself to feel any of the satisfaction coursing through me.

We'd done it.

We were going to the monsters' ball.

Then I stumbled, shaken by the sudden realization that not all of the exultation I felt actually belonged to me.

It was Reese's.

His emotions were filling me up, as if they were my own.

More vampire mind-control.

# Chapter 21

"Come on." Grabbing Reese by the sleeve, I tugged him more quickly toward the exit.

Once again, the vampires melted away from us.

The whispers started before we made it all the way to the door. "Claimed," I heard, over and over.

I pulled Reese through the foyer and slammed the door behind us. "What happened in there?" I demanded as soon as we were outside. "What did you do to me? Why was I able to throw Dahlia around like that? Why can I feel you, in my head, in my stomach, everywhere?"

"I don't know." Reese held his hands out as if to ward me off. "This is like nothing I've ever felt before."

"Liar. You Claimed me tonight, didn't you? That's what you were doing when you told Mendoza to back off, isn't it?" He was backed up against the redbrick wall, and I was right in his face.

"Um. Maybe?" he said.

"You sneaky, lying, son of a bitch...vampire!" I spit out the word, unable to think of any worse term.

"I mean it—this is new for me too. I didn't do it on purpose. I didn't even know that's what I was doing." He slid around me, moving so he faced me on the sidewalk.

"But it's what you did. Without ever even asking me. What if I don't want to be Claimed? What if I don't want to get stuck with a fucking vampire for the rest of my life?" I was shouting now.

"I don't think that's how it works," Reese said in a quiet voice.

"Then maybe you'd like to tell me how it does work, since you're such an expert." I stormed down the street, hoping for a taxi to come by.

"I don't think the human gets to choose. You just get Claimed. The vampire does the Claiming."

"Oh!" I nearly screeched in frustration. "You get to choose? Why don't I get to choose? How about this? I Claim you, Reese." What had the magic words been? "My Claim, my blood!" I shouted the last words at the top of my voice.

A window flew open in another building and someone yelled, "Shut up, lady!"

I wasn't listening, though. I was too busy dealing with my body's reaction to what I'd announced.

It was like getting punched in the stomach. All the breath flew out of me and I collapsed to my knees, clutching my abdomen. Stars of pain floated in front of my eyes, bright sparks on black velvet. When they cleared, I looked around and saw Reese huddled against the brick wall of a nearby building, mouth working like a gaping fish but no sound coming out.

The thread between us was almost palpable, not quite silver or ringing or burning, yet overwhelming all of my senses with its bright invisibility.

"Oh," I moaned. "No."

*No, no, no. What have I done?*

But I had a pretty good idea what I'd done.

Claimed Reese.

Even if it wasn't supposed to be possible.

Double damn and hellfire.

This was not turning out to be one of my better evenings.

I walked back over to Reese and pulled his arm so it draped around my shoulder, heaving him up until he was almost standing. "Come on," I said. He staggered down the street with me, turning bleary eyes to meet mine.

"Well," he rasped. "That's a hell of a note."

# Chapter 22

"Did you know you were being promoted to Dallas administrator tonight?" I asked as I guided Reese toward his pickup.

"No, of course not," Reese said. He was beginning to perk up, taking more of his own weight, staggering less and walking more. He stopped on the sidewalk and turned to face me. "I do not want any part of the administration." He turned back around and started walking again.

I didn't move. "You told Mendoza you wanted in."

"That was part of our cover, a way to learn more. I don't want to be a member of the Sanguinary. I want to wipe them out. That's all. The end."

"Why?"

He stopped again, but this time he didn't turn around to face me. "Why what?"

"Why do you want to take out the Sanguinary?" I asked. "I don't think the recent murders are all that's motivating you. Maybe not even the possibility of shutting down the portals."

His shoulders lifted and lowered in what I assumed was a sigh.

When he didn't answer immediately, I groped around with those senses that weren't really senses, feeling my way along the connection between us as I searched for something in particular. "This is more personal," I said.

"Stop it," he said. "I'll tell you. Just quit digging around in my head."

We reached his pickup and he handed me the keys, leaning back against the tailgate and closing his eyes. "I had a bloodgiver once. Leila. The Sanguinary killed her."

I didn't have to search across our connection any longer. His emotions, dark and painful, shot through the link, punching me in the stomach and bringing tears to my eyes. "How?" My voice sounded small, lost in the misery pulsing from him in waves.

"They drained her. Took her in a blood house, against all the rules, and drained her. Used her in one of their rituals to open a portal."

"Oh, Jesus," I whispered. "Were you…was she Claimed?"

"Yes."

At the word, jealousy spiked through my chest, hot and fast, and Reese jerked, opening his eyes to stare at me. I pushed the unwelcome emotion back down, but it was too late. Reese had felt it too.

That didn't mean we had to acknowledge it, though.

"Do you know which Sanguinary member actually killed her?" I asked, working to maintain a calm appearance, no matter how I felt.

Reese nodded. "Dahlia," he said. He growled the name.

"Why haven't you done something already?" I asked.

"Because I know she wasn't the only one involved. And I want to take all of them down." Our bond shivered with his snarl.

Despite my best intentions, I couldn't keep the questions from swirling through my mind. Had his connection to Leila been this strong?

Had she felt his every emotion? Had he felt hers?

Had he felt her die?

He shook his head, answering my unspoken questions. "It wasn't like this. Whatever we have is…different. Something new. It's like nothing I've ever heard of." His voice roughened with something akin to desire, and his eyes began to glow. Heat pooled deep in my belly, and I couldn't tell if the feeling was my own, or if it came from Reese.

Crap. We were both far too vulnerable to one another's responses. We had to get out of here, go somewhere private to figure out what the hell had happened to us when I announced my Claim on him.

"Okay," I said breathlessly. "The Sanguinary needs to be taken down. I'm with you. But first we've got to deal with this Claiming business."

"Agreed. My place still? I'll drive."

Reese may have sounded a little stronger now, but I still didn't trust him behind the wheel. "No way in hell, cowboy. You gave me the keys. I'm the designated driver."

\* \* \*

Rather to my surprise, Reese lived in an art gallery. Through the front window, I could see large canvases hung in tasteful arrangements on the walls.

"This way." Reese stepped away from the truck and unlocked a side door leading into a small hallway, and I followed him back to an office. The room had an expensive-looking desk, several leather chairs, and a matching leather couch. It also had another door that led, I presumed, into the rest of the gallery.

I wandered around for a moment, and discovered I was right: lots of fancy art in the front, offices in the back.

The smell of coffee drew me back to Reese's office. Silently, he handed me a cup.

I took a sip and leaned back in the chair I had chosen. I was staying away from sofas for a while, I had decided. At least while Reese was around.

"So what do you think happened back there?" I finally asked.

He shook his head. "I don't know. But I don't feel any more powerful. Just more…connected."

I grimaced at the understatement.

"Me too. But I wasn't even trying to hurt Dahlia." My neck and breasts were beginning to ache a little where he'd bitten them too. Not that I would tell him that. Or show anyone else.

Vampire bite marks—more embarrassing than the worst hickey ever.

His glance suggested that he knew exactly what I was feeling.

"Maybe we should try an experiment," I said. "See if you got anything special out of the Claiming."

"Like what?"

"I don't know. Like…" I searched my memory for things that an uber-strong vampire might be able to do. For all my years on the Sucker Squad, I didn't know much more about vampires than how to kill them. All I could come up with were scenes from old movies. "Try to turn into a bat."

"What?"

"You know. Small, flying, nocturnal creature. Uses sonar to navigate."

"I know what a bat is, smartass." Reese shook his head.

"Then try to turn into one."

"I wouldn't even know where to start."

"Close your eyes and imagine what it's like to be a bat." I mimicked wing flutters with my hands.

"Fine." Reese closed his eyes. We both sat in silence for a minute.

"You're not changing," I said.

"I didn't think I was."

"There's not even a little bit of mist or anything. Try harder."

Reese opened one eye to look at me. "I don't really want to be a bat."

"What do you want to be?"

"I'm fine being me." He took a drink of his coffee.

"Dammit. I need you to take this seriously. You said humans aren't supposed to be able to Claim vampires at all. Is that because no one's ever tried, or because it shouldn't be possible?"

He shook his head. "I don't know."

I kept talking, running over his words with my own. "And if it's not possible, why did it happen with us? What can we do with it? Is it a weakness? A strength?"

Reese leaned forward to clasp my hands in his own cool, dry ones, stopping my litany of increasingly hysterical-sounding questions with his quiet words. "We'll try again."

I drew in a shaky breath. "Okay."

He continued holding my hands as he closed his eyes, absent-mindedly stroking his thumbs across my wrists.

This time, I felt something in the bond between us, like flickers of light dancing along a wire.

"Keep going," I whispered.

The flickers intensified, like hot wax dripping onto me, then flames licking across my skin, sending shivers trembling across my body. Within moments, heat poured through me, pulsing across every inch of my skin.

Reese's glowing blue eyes popped open, his gaze boring into mine. Sheer, raw power swirled inside me, and then rushed through our clasped hands, pouring into him in waves. The transfer didn't last for more than a few seconds, but left me gasping with something between pain and pleasure, my senses reeling from the power transfer.

We stared at each other for a long, silent moment, until Reese stood up. As he unclasped my hands, I realized that his grasp had grown as warm as if he had recently fed.

"I don't know what that was, but I still didn't turn into a bat." A shaky smile highlighted his own uncertain reaction.

I was about to suggest that he try shifting into a wolf when I heard a strange, arrhythmic thumping noise from outside the room.

"What is that?" I asked.

We both listened for a moment. It was like nothing I'd ever heard before. But the screeching that came along with it gave me a pretty good idea of what it might be.

"Wait here," Reese said. "I'll go check it out."

He stepped out of the office and into the hall, the noise increasing in frequency as he opened the door. I trailed along behind him and stood in the doorway, listening, poised to run in case it was something horrible.

I wasn't entirely certain if I planned to run toward Reese, or away from him.

"Hey, Cami? I think you need to come see this," Reese called from the front gallery.

I only made it a few feet into the showroom before I froze. I'd been right. Bats, blindly beating their tiny wings against the windows. Hundreds and hundreds of bats.

"Damn," I breathed.

"That's one way of putting it," Reese said. We both stared at the windows, transfixed by the sight.

"Reese? Whatever you do, don't think about turning into a wolf."

"Hadn't planned on it." His voice was wry.

"Think you can get rid of them?" I asked.

"I don't know. But I'm certainly going to try." He closed his eyes for a moment. The bats slowly stopped beating their wings, and began clutching the tops of the windows and hanging upside down.

"They're not gone," I said.

"I know that. Hush. I'm trying to concentrate."

I had to work pretty hard not to keep narrating. But I bit my tongue—figuratively this time, as it was still a bit sore from the piercing it had gotten earlier. And after a few moments of silence, the bats slowly began drifting away from the window, back, I presumed, to their normal little batty lives.

"They're gone," I finally whispered.

Reese opened his eyes. "Okay," he said. "That was weird."

"Thank you, Mr. Understatement."

"You know what?" Reese said. "I think that's about all the experimentation I'm up for tonight." His voice sounded strained. He went back to his office and sat down on a sofa. I followed him.

"So." I let the word stretch out as I folded myself into the chair across from him. "What are we going to do?"

"To be honest, sugar, I didn't know these kinds of things existed. I didn't think it was possible for a vampire to call bats. Or for a human to Claim a vampire."

"Well, clearly you were wrong." I shook my head and sighed. "Isn't there some sort of, I don't know, vampire divorce for these kinds of things?"

"Is it really all that bad?" Reese said. "I mean, look at how you dealt with Dahlia. That kind of strength might come in handy in a fight."

"Reese, I don't marry vampires. I kill them."

*And have sex with one of them, apparently, but I'm not going to bring that up right now.*

"We're not married," he said.

"No? If being tied together for the rest of our lives—well, my life, anyway—isn't exactly like the worst marriage ever, then I don't know what is."

He closed his eyes again. "I don't know, Cami. I don't have any answers right now."

My shoulders slumped. I had really been hoping that Reese would have something slick to say. I'd held on to the hope during the whole drive back to his place, even as I knew deep in my heart that this was all new to him too.

"So what now?" I asked softly. "Do we simply move ahead? Does this Claiming business change anything?"

"I think maybe it changes everything," Reese said.

"This is different from your other Claimings?" I tried to stay calm and reasonable, even managing to keep my tone even, but sheer terror was clawing its way up my throat.

"It is." Opening his eyes, he stared at me intently. "But I don't think you need to be afraid of it."

"You just called a whole colony of bats to your front window by thinking about it. I'm all kinds of afraid."

"I mean about Halloween. Does this change our strategy?"

"Oh. That. Not really. Not unless you think of some way to use this."

I didn't say it aloud, but I knew that I would be doing my best to avoid thinking of this whole Claiming thing at all.

I took a deep breath. "Okay, then. Day after tomorrow is the Halloween ball. You'll come pick me up?"

He nodded.

"Good. I'm going home now."

"I'll take you," Reese said.

"No, thanks." I pulled out my cell phone. "I think I'll call a cab tonight."

"Are you sure?"

"Yeah. I'll see you on Halloween, okay?" I needed the time until then to get ready—and maybe come to terms with the fact that I was connected, perhaps permanently, to a vampire.

Reese nodded. "Okay. Good night, Cami."

"Good night, Reese." We both stood there awkwardly for a moment, but then I unlocked the front door and left.

I could still feel him watching me as I got into the cab.

As the car pulled away from the curb, I watched a solitary bat swooping back and forth across the gallery display window.

# Chapter 23

I woke the next morning thinking of the question of how we were going to use our newfound power to our advantage—just exactly as I had said I wouldn't.

I considered possible answers to that question all day long.

A phone conference with Iverson and Captain James solidified our strategy, including the SWAT team's role.

Plans in place, I shopped for my perfect ball gown. I was discovering that it really wasn't that easy to describe to salespeople what I was looking for. "A dress with a nice big skirt to hide my gun, some shoes to hide stakes in, and a good spot for a really sharp knife" doesn't inspire trust, somehow.

I did finally find it, though. I love Dallas—you can find everything here if you're willing to look long enough. In a tiny bridal boutique, I found a stunning dress. It had a full, blood-red skirt, perfect for hiding small weapons, and a tight black bodice with simple straps.

"Do you do alterations?" I asked the flamboyantly gay man who had been helping me. "And can you get them done by tomorrow afternoon?"

"Of course, darling, for the right price. What do you want done?"

*Hmm. How to put this?*

"I need some…loops added. To hold things."

He nodded. "Of course. You bring everything in and we'll take care of it for you."

"Actually, I've got some right here." I dug around in my purse and found two stakes of different length. "I want a loop for this one inside here," I said, slipping the stake under the skirt. The salesman's eyes widened, but he nodded.

"No problem," he said.

"And I want spots for these here, here, and here." I flipped the stakes from spot to spot, demonstrating which ones I thought might fit inside the folds of the dress. "Whatever will look most natural."

"Of course. We can have the dress by closing."

Wow, that was easy. Of course, it should have been easy for what I paid for the dress. The least they could do was alter it a little. And not ask any questions.

I left the two stakes with the salesman so their seamstress could size the loops, and went hunting for shoes next. I carried with me a tiny swatch of the dress's fabric cut from an inside seam. I finally found a matching sandal much like the one Reese had bought for me: medium heel, with a satin ankle wrap I could use to strap more stakes to my ankle. Nothing like a flirty shoe with a hidden stake to make a girl feel like a princess. I also found a matching satin wrap and sequin-encrusted purse. I was ready for my big night.

If only it were that easy to prepare myself mentally.

# Chapter 24

Halloween morning dawned bright and cool. I woke at sunrise, too wired to sleep any longer, despite the fact that I'd had a difficult time sleeping all night.

My dress and accessories hung from my closet door—my apartment looked like a high school girl's room right before prom. The dress was fitted with all the stakes it could hold—a surprising number. The seamstress at the dress shop had done an amazing job of hiding stakes everywhere the dress folded or bunched, including several in the hem. If I hadn't known better, I would have said she'd sewn weapons into dresses before.

At any rate, I'd gotten her card after I'd seen the amazing work she did. If I survived the night, I would be requesting her services again.

The purse and the wrap hung in plastic beside the dress.

If I concentrated, I could still tell where—and how—he was, more or less.

To the south, not awake.

I tried not to concentrate on it, because it creeped me out.

I looked out my window, enjoying the feel of the late-fall sun on my face. That's when I noticed the package on the outside sill, wrapped in dark red paper. A light coat of dew had settled on it, darkening the bow and making it droop. An envelope was taped to the box. I opened the window and carefully removed the card, trying not to disturb the box. I'd hate to get blown up by a bomb.

The envelope had a card inside, dark red to match the wrapping paper. Inside the card, it read: *Did I mention this is a masquerade? See you at ten. —R*

Reese must have left it while I was sleeping.

Did that mean that he could tell when I was sleeping, just as I could tell when he was?

I pulled the gift into my room and opened it. Inside was a mask, reminiscent of the Mardi Gras masks I'd seen on visits to New Orleans, designed to fit over the eyes and the bridge of the nose. All across the mask swirled delicate whorls of dark red lace.

It matched my dress perfectly.

Of course.

It occurred to me that in order to know what color my dress was, Reese must have been spying on me, but I pushed the thought away. It was quickly followed by the realization that he might have been spying on me through my own eyes, seeing the dress through me, as I had seen the crowds in the blood house through him.

That thought wasn't as easily banished as the first.

Under the mask sat two hair clips, painted to match the mask. And connected to each clip was a small wooden stake, designed, when the clip was attached, to be hidden in the wearer's hair.

I smiled and set the mask and clips gently down on the dresser.

I spent most of the day getting ready for the ball as if it were a regular party. I got a manicure and pedicure at the tiny salon around the corner. Then I went to Rosie two shops down to get my hair put up. She'd been recommended by one of the SMU sorority girls who lived in my building—I'd asked when we'd been in the laundry room the day before. I assumed anyone who wore T-shirts emblazoned with ZTA would know where to get a good up-do.

So by 9:45 that night, I was ready. I looked good too. Much better than any woman set on killing a bunch of vampires has any right to. The fitted top of the dress pulled in my waist like a corset, pushing my breasts up and making me look much curvier than I actually was. The pinprick marks from Reese's teeth were almost gone, leaving only a hint of a dark shadow—no one would notice the marks unless he or she were looking for them.

Of course, at a vampire party, people might be looking.

The neck and shoulder wounds were more obvious, but if I arranged my wrap correctly, they, too, were hidden.

My sequined purse held a tiny, pearl-handled derringer Garrett had given me as a gift one Christmas. It was loaded with two rounds of the new anti-vamp ammo.

I had an audio device shoved deep into my ear. Every so often, Tech One or Tech Two would say something—or Iverson would check in with some inane comment.

They didn't know what had transpired between Reese and me. And since I didn't exactly know, either, I wanted to keep it that way. I was thankful for the veneer of normalcy they lent this insane plan.

If they knew I had some crazy vampire-Claiming mojo, they might back out.

I stood by my door, waiting impatiently. At precisely ten o'clock, Reese knocked on the door.

"We're on," I said quietly.

"Ten-four," Iverson replied. "Everyone is in place, Cinderella. You'll have until midnight at the ball, unless you give the signal earlier. Don't leave any shoes behind."

"Very funny." Still, it was good to know the SWAT team was in place, waiting for our signal.

I opened the door, wrap in hand. Reese stood outside, his face mostly covered by a black silk mask, his hair brushed back so that it barely touched his collar.

Even with his face covered, he looked unbelievably good in a tuxedo.

I pushed that thought aside too. I was getting awfully good at pushing aside thoughts.

"Okay," I said. "Let's go."

"It's nice to see you too," he said.

I sighed. "Sorry. I'm a little on edge." And I didn't really want to look him in the eye, given our last encounter and the wire in my ear.

"You look lovely." He placed his fingertips gently under my chin and tipped my face up toward him. "The dress suits you."

I pulled my face away from his hand.

"The mask is a lovely gift. It matches my dress perfectly. Thank you," I said, gesturing toward my ear.

Reese nodded and clasped his hands behind his back. "I see."

He had a limousine waiting downstairs for us. The driver didn't look like a vampire, so I assumed Reese had hired him through a regular service. In the back seat, Reese handed me a glass of Champagne.

"Thanks," I said, "but I don't plan to drink tonight."

"I guessed as much. Sparkling grape juice for you," he said.

We rode along in silence for a while. When Reese finally spoke, his voice was soft. "I met with Mendoza earlier tonight. He gave me the rundown on my induction into the Sanguinary."

My breath caught in my throat. "Did he actually say that?"

"Yes. They're planning to introduce me publicly as the new Dallas admin. Then later tonight, there is supposed to be a smaller, private ceremony." His gaze bored into mine, his voice growing increasingly intense. "There will be Sanguinary members from all over the country there tonight, Cami. We won't just take down the Dallas Sanguinary. We'll cripple the entire organization."

I nodded. "Good."

Feigning a calm I didn't feel, I sipped my drink until we pulled up in front of the Adolphus Hotel downtown, its red brick looming over us. As I climbed out of the limo, I tilted my head back to look at the baroque facade, and could barely make out the gargoyles leering down at us.

The building itself was red brick part of the way up, then white stone for the final several stories. The detailed window arches reminded me of an older, more graceful time. A red carpet had been rolled from the entry to the street. There weren't any cameras flashing, but a group of gawkers had gathered to gape at the beautiful people arriving in limos and stepping into the building.

I wanted to tell the tourists to run away, that these were not really people—they were the creepy, undead Sanguinary who would enslave humans and use them as pets and meals.

But more than I wanted to warn them, I didn't want to get kicked out before the party started.

So, instead, I moved under the black awning, took Reese's arm, and strolled into the building, ignoring the tourists and their gawking.

*I'm the one walking into a room full of blood-sucking fiends. The tourists are probably safer.*

I had to admit, though, that it was a beautiful setting for a room full of blood-sucking fiends.

We slowly followed the line of people from the lobby, wending our way up the sweeping staircase toward the main ballroom.

Looking ahead, I realized why we were all moving so slowly. There was some sort of receiving line at the top of the stairs.

Unlike the guests, none of the vampires in the reception line were masked. Mendoza was first, of course, followed by Boyd—without his wan human, I noticed—and two other vampires I had never met. One of them was a woman, tall and beautiful in a typically vampy-gorgeous way.

The other was a small man with a dark, old-fashioned mustache that curled up at the ends. In his formal wear, he looked like a villain out of an old melodrama—like he should have a top hat and cane, and be busy tying beautiful young women to railroad tracks. Even if he hadn't been in the receiving line, I probably would have marked him as a vampire based on looks alone.

They all murmured polite greetings. I smiled and tried to ignore the press of their dead, cold flesh against my hand.

Mendoza brushed a kiss across the back of my hand and said, "It's good to see you here."

I managed not to shudder.

By 10:45, we were through the receiving line and inside the ballroom. Crystal chandeliers glittered, almost obscuring the gorgeous trompe l'oeil celestial paintings. At the far end of the room, a dais stood in front of long, burgundy velvet drapes. Music drifted across the room from the small orchestra playing near the dance floor. The ballroom was easily three or four times as big as the blood house, but it was every bit as crowded—which explained why Mendoza hadn't wanted to hold his party in the blood house itself.

There were probably several hundred vampires here.

*I'm a dead woman.*

Therefore, I was determined to enjoy myself for at least part of this party.

Not that I wouldn't enjoy the killing-vampires part. I would.

But first I was going enjoy my lovely new party dress for the short span of the rest of its—and probably my—life.

"So," said Reese, "where shall we start?"

"Actually," I said, "I'd like to start with a dance. This is the first real ball I've ever been to, and I'd hate for the killing to start before I got to dance."

Reese shook his head and began laughing. "You never cease to surprise me, Cami Davis." Taking my hand, he led me to the dance floor, spinning me into his arms.

We danced several sets—my favorite, though, was the waltz. Reese was an expert dancer, sweeping me lightly across the dance floor. And for the space of those three or four dances, I was able to pretend, for a short while, that this was a normal party, a regular date. That I was a normal woman out with a normal man, and we were having a normal evening.

I don't know how long I would have gone on pretending if Iverson's voice hadn't finally sounded in my ear.

"Okay, Cinderella, we've got you on video. Repeat: Video is up and running. We're waiting for the rest of the attendees to arrive."

"Okay," I murmured.

If Iverson had eyes in the ballroom, then we were almost ready. My job was to mark the vamps for the team, to help them try to avoid killing the humans. The people in league with vampires were probably acceptable casualties, if it came down to it. But there were other people in the hotel, and we didn't want to take out any of them, if we could help it.

This could end up being a worse bloodbath than the clinic.

"Time to get going here," I said to Reese. "Introduce me to anyone you think is a Sanguinary member. Pretend you're glad-handing it as the new Dallas admin," I said.

*And please don't really be taking the job. Please be on my side for real.*

"You got it." Reese scanned the room for a moment.

Everywhere, vampires and humans in luxurious evening wear and exotic masks mingled, the hum of conversation and the clinking of crystal glasses providing a steady undertone to the music provided by the orchestra tucked into a corner of the room.

"Okay," Reese finally said. "Let's begin over there, with the couple in the matching blue masks."

As we made our way around the room, I realized that Reese really was a consummate politician. He knew everyone, and everyone knew him. They watched me with wary eyes, though, and I realized that there must be stories about me circulating through the vampire community. I even caught the tail end of a few whispered conversations: "killed him for touching her," "Reese's Claim," "threw her across the room," "Reese's power." And through it all, I smiled and shook hands, touched vampires on the arm, the shoulder, the small of the back.

It was exhausting. I hadn't realized how difficult it would be to make conversation with the vampires I was planning to execute.

Worse, I actually liked some of them. A blonde woman in a green dress had confided to me that she'd always wondered why Reese hadn't taken a companion and said she was glad to see him finally "come into his own." A tall, gangly man in a tuxedo with too-short arms had tripped over his own words until he had started talking about his quest to synthesize human blood. He reminded me of the less-articulate crime-scene techs, socially hopeless but brilliant when in their own element.

I had to keep reminding myself that these were all vampires.

They were all connected to the Sanguinary, all part of a group of vampires who would happily see humanity enslaved, turned into blood-giving pets.

None of these vampires were of the "good" variety.

If there were even any such thing as a good vampire.

I looked over at Reese out of the corner of my eye. He was smiling at an anecdote a young-looking vampire was telling about a recent blood house party. I wondered what thoughts Reese's urbane smile hid, then wondered if I could figure out his thoughts if I concentrated hard enough.

Worried what I might discover, I decided not to try.

*Snap out of it, Davis,* I admonished myself silently. *This is no time to start worrying about Reese. Think of him as a coworker.* I could deal with that stuff after we got through the night. If we got through the night.

I shook my head and Reese glanced down at me with a frown. A spark skittered across my skin, as if trying to find a way in. I scanned the room for something to distract my vampire partner.

Across the room, Leah Richards gestured with her mask to emphasize a point as she spoke to Dahlia, whose back was toward me.

Where was Garrett?

"I'll be back," I said to Reese.

He followed my gaze and nodded. "Have fun."

I made my way over to the pair, coming up behind Dahlia and putting my hand on her back.

"Dahlia, darling," I purred into her ear.

She jumped away from my hand and Richards laughed.

"Don't touch me, you freak," Dahlia's little-girl voice was even more highly pitched than usual.

"Where's my ex-partner?" I glanced around for Garrett.

"Oh, I've got a surprise for you tonight." Dahlia tried to drop her voice down to a more silky tone. "I've arranged for him to be here later."

*This can't be good.*

"Or maybe he isn't here because you just couldn't hold his attention," I said, trying to simultaneously survey the room for my former partner.

*Where is he? What the hell did Dahlia mean?*

"I don't have to listen to this," Dahlia pouted.

"No," said Richards, "you could get your ass tossed across the room. What do you think?" she asked, turning to me. "Are you up for another round of Toss the Vampire Bitch?"

Dahlia's nostrils flared and her eyes narrowed. She hissed wordlessly at Richards and stalked off.

"That was fabulous," I said, watching Dahlia go.

Richards hit my wrist with her mask. "Just because I don't like Dahlia doesn't mean that I do like you. Don't think I'm going to forget that." She strode away.

"Fine," I muttered. "Wait till you get your ass staked."

"What was that?" Iverson said in my ear.

"Nothing." I moved back to Reese, who watched my return with amusement dancing in his eyes. We continued our rounds, meeting up eventually with Boyd and his gaunt bloodgiver, who had joined him after all. Seeing him up close, I realized that the vampire had been a small man in life. He wasn't even as tall as I was. He was clearly one of those little men who hated his women to be taller than him—his bloodgiver was tiny, barely reaching Boyd's shoulder.

"Reese," he said in greeting. "I understand you are to be nominated for the Dallas administrator position." The cold anger in his gaze left no doubt: He disliked being passed over for the position.

"It's not official yet." Reese's nonconfrontational tone was at odds with the way he stepped closer to Boyd, looming over him threateningly.

"These things rarely are beforehand." Boyd spoke through clenched teeth. "I have a few concerns I'd like to discuss with you as soon as possible."

Both vampires were ignoring me, so I sidled up to Boyd's bloodgiver. She looked pale and wan and miserable, following her vampire around. "Hi," I said, holding out my hand. "I'm Cami."

The woman looked at me with huge, terrified eyes. I was about to say something else—I don't know what, but I was aiming for something soothing—when Boyd turned around and hissed at me. Not in words—it was another one of those creepy vampire hisses. He bared his fangs, and with a snarl, snatched his bloodgiver away from me.

"You should train your pets to behave in public," he hissed. "And not to speak when her betters are talking."

I gasped in outrage. But Reese smiled and said, "I'm perfectly happy with her behavior, Boyd."

"And this is exactly why you should not be named administrator." Grabbing the woman by the hand, he stalked off.

I hoped he didn't survive the night, and that his bloodgiver got good professional help when it was all over.

The closer we got to midnight, the more nervous I felt. I kept touching vampires, hoping Iverson and his crew were taking careful notes.

At five minutes until midnight, right as I thought my nerves were close to the breaking point, Mendoza stepped out onto the raised dais at the far end of the room.

"Friends, loved ones, guests," he said loudly. Everyone turned to look at him and the hum of conversation slowly died down.

"It's a pleasure to see you all here tonight." He nodded toward the back of the room, and two tuxedoed vampires swung the ballroom doors closed.

"The room is locked down," Iverson's tinny voice in my ear reported.

"Wait!" I hissed. People near us turned their heads to find the disturbance. I quickly glanced at Reese, hoping it would look like I was speaking to him. "I want to hear this," I whispered.

"We're on hold," Iverson said. "The code word for 'go' is *pineapple*. Repeat: *pineapple*."

*Pineapple?*

On the small stage, Mendoza had finished his greetings and moved on. "At a traditional Venetian masked ball," he said, "it is usual to unmask at midnight and go to the dining room for a late supper."

Everyone was staring at Mendoza with rapt attention.

"However, we do not have a late supper, nor could many of us eat one even if we did—" And here he paused for a moment. When the crowd had stopped laughing politely, he continued, "So let us all remove our masks, shall we?"

There was a rustling noise as the crowd obeyed.

"Now," Mendoza said, "I have arranged not for a light midnight supper, but rather, for a sumptuous feast—and a glorious passage."

With a flourish, he signaled to someone behind the curtains that were blocking off the back part of the room. The fabric pulled aside to reveal a small, raised stage holding maybe thirty or forty people—human people—huddled together, blinking into the spotlight now turned on them. The crowd gasped in delight and began applauding wildly.

"Holy Mary, Mother of God," Iverson whispered into my ear. "Is that what I think it is?"

"The big sacrifice," I answered grimly.

The people on the stage were chained together, and many of them wore hospital-style nightgowns. Those who were wearing civilian clothes stood out clearly. And there, right in the middle of the group, chained with the rest of the feast, was Agent Stan Chandler.

"Oh, no," I said.

"We'll get them out of here," Reese whispered.

Staring at the group on the stage, I tried to figure out how we were going to carry out our original plan without hurting any of these people. Although I hadn't been happy with the idea of human casualties, I had been okay with the knowledge that a few of the vampires' human buddies might die in this operation. It was, I rationalized, the price you risked paying for hanging out with creatures of the night.

But these people had not chosen to be here. They were innocent victims.

And one of them was FBI.

# Chapter 25

"I would like to thank the Alfred Ellison Psychiatric Institute for its generous donation tonight," Mendoza was saying as he gestured toward the group of chained people, many of whom were now openly crying.

Crap. There was more than one clinic under the vampires' control.

The patients shifted a bit, shuffling on the stage. Vampire guards stood on either side of them, watching the victims carefully.

Then I froze as another one of the chained victims caught my eye.

Garrett.

Dahlia's surprise.

I should have thrown her across the room again when I had the chance. *I will kill her the next time I see her.*

Mendoza continued, "But before we begin dinner, I have a few announcements to make."

"I can save those people," Reese whispered. "Follow my lead."

Follow his lead? That wasn't the plan.

"Cami," Iverson said in my ear. "Are we on?"

"Not yet." I wasn't willing to let the killing start until I knew what Reese was planning.

And whose side he was really on.

Reese made his way toward the dais, and I followed him. Mendoza, searching the crowd, made eye contact with Reese and smiled.

*Oh, God. Please let me be right about Reese.*

"As many of you know," Mendoza said, "the post of North Texas administrator was recently left open. I have been asked to take, and have accepted, that post." Polite applause. "The Cabinet has met, and has decided to appoint Reese Fulton to my former position as Dallas administrator. Reese, would you step up here please?" Mendoza held his hand out toward Reese, and someone aimed a spotlight directly on us, blinding me momentarily. I blinked the dazzle away, squinting toward the dais and the stage behind it.

At that moment, Garrett looked up and made eye contact with me, anguish flooding his face. Before I could even acknowledge him, give him some signal to tell him we would free him, he let out a howl and leapt toward Mendoza.

I don't know what he planned to do, what he thought he could accomplish, chained as he was to other victims, surrounded by vampires.

He was pale—weak from his addiction, from blood loss. From misery.

Maybe he hoped to take down even one of the bastards who had brought him to this state. But he didn't have a weapon, didn't have anyone backing him up. As he jumped toward Mendoza, another vampire reached out, almost casually, and snapped his neck.

Garrett crumpled to the floor, pulling several of the people chained to him down to their knees around him.

Mendoza gestured at one of his lackeys, who pulled out a knife and knelt next to my partner's body.

"Well," Mendoza said in a horribly jovial tone, "I guess we will begin the festivities early."

As I stood frozen in the middle of the ballroom, the vampire leader spoke a few words in a language I didn't understand. A blue light gathered around Garrett's body, shining through what looked like a hole in the air.

"Hold that open," Mendoza directed the vampire who had pulled open Garrett's shirt and was carving something into his abdomen with a knife.

Symbols that matched the ones on the Vamp Killer's vics.

Reese was right: The Sanguinary was using clinic patients—and now my former partner—to open a hole between worlds.

I didn't want to see what was on the other side of that passage.

I couldn't let Mendoza get any further in his plan. I tensed, preparing to jump. But then Reese leaned over and kissed my cheek, squeezing my hand tightly. "Do not react," he whispered. I did my best to make my expression blank—to avoid looking at Garrett's lifeless body being carved into on the stage, even as his empty, open eyes seemed to stare at me accusingly.

I tried not to think that in his last moments, he had believed he was truly alone.

*I won't just kill Dahlia. I will make her suffer first.*

Reese let go of my hand and moved, smiling and waving triumphantly as he made his way onto the dais, ignoring Garrett's death as if it had not occurred.

As if it didn't matter.

As the spotlight followed him, I blinked again and looked past the stage, right into Stan Chandler's furious eyes.

Clearly Reese's mind-meld trick at the blood house hadn't completely worked. The FBI agent had persevered in his questions, at least enough to get him picked up by the Sanguinary.

And now he thought I had something to do with him ending up chained to a group of other victims in the Adolphus Hotel ballroom.

If we both lived, I'd set him straight. Eventually. Right now, I had more important issues to deal with.

As Reese arrived at the middle of the stage, Mendoza reached out and grasped his hand, raising it above his head in a sign of victory. Reese smiled broadly.

*No, no, no. Please don't be one of them.* The almost-prayer ran through my mind over and over.

Then their hands came down and Reese turned in toward Mendoza, pulling him close and whispering something in his ear.

When they parted, it looked for a moment like nothing untoward had happened—other, of course, than my sometimes-boyfriend vampire partner taking over a major Texas city and preparing to open a portal to some kind of hellish vampire dimension.

But then Mendoza staggered back a couple of steps and blood bloomed through a ragged hole in his white shirt, staining the front and dripping to the floor.

I hadn't seen that coming.

Everyone froze for a moment, as if trying to comprehend the idea that Reese, new administration member, had actually staked Mendoza, one of the most important vampires in the Sanguinary.

Follow his lead, he'd said.

Okay, then.

I drew in a deep breath, and then…

"Pineapple!" I shouted at the top of my voice.

All around me, the vampires I had marked began having difficulty keeping their heads, courtesy of Iverson's snipers.

As soon as I saw the first bloody pop, I ran for the dais, pushing against the general tide of the crowd, most of whom were headed for the exits.

As I waded upstream through the mob of people, I pulled a stake out of its loop down inside my cleavage. Every chance I got, I took a vampire down with it. It was easier than I had expected—many vampires were still trying to figure out exactly what was going on.

My main goal, though, was to get up on the stage. I got a glimpse of it through the crowd and saw that Chandler—or someone, anyway—had gotten everyone to lie down when the shooting started.

Good for him. I hoped he could keep all those poor people calm until I got there.

As I moved across the room, a female vamp—the blonde in the green dress who had been so nice earlier—jumped me, her hands curled into claws aiming for my eyes, her mouth open wide as she let out a bloodcurdling scream.

I didn't even have to think about it. I pulled with my mind, and I could feel Reese's strength flow through me.

I punched my fist out toward the vampire's stomach and caught her in mid-air, sending her flying up toward the ceiling, still shrieking incoherently.

A sudden pop silenced her screech. I got one look at her eyes, wide with surprise, and then her head exploded in a shower of evil-smelling vampire blood and brains, raining down all over my beautiful new dress.

I shook a clump of brain matter off my hand. It landed on the floor with a plop.

I glanced behind me to see Iverson, his eyes huge, leaning against the doorframe, holding his gun steady with both hands, still aiming where the vamp had been. He held my gaze for a long moment and I froze, waiting for his response to my action. Finally, he nodded at me once, solemnly. I waved my thanks and raced toward the stage.

Reese was already there, trying to talk to the prisoners as I clambered up some side stairs.

Unfortunately for Reese, most of the prisoners were patients from a psychiatric institute.

One of them was standing with his arms high in the air, dragging the people chained directly to him in so close that their hands raised with his—which made him look oddly like a prophet surrounded by adoring acolytes—and screaming, "The end is nigh! The apocalypse is upon us!" over and over at the top of his voice.

"You don't know how right you are, buddy," I muttered, moving to the side to try to find a curtain pull. We needed a little distance from the carnage to keep these people safe.

There wasn't a curtain cord—it must have been controlled from some central area—but luckily for me, I could pull the curtains closed by hand. So I did exactly that, running across the front of the stage and hoping that no one out in the ballroom would decide to start shooting through the curtain blindly.

I turned and surveyed the group. For a brief moment, I stared down at Garrett's body. The strange blue light emanating from him had disappeared at some point, leaving only his open-eyed corpse. I bent down long enough to close his eyes. "I'm sorry, partner," I whispered.

Then I moved back to the group of people and knelt down next to Chandler. "How are you doing?" I asked him, hoping to distract him while I figured out how to get all these people safely out of the ballroom.

"A little confused," he said.

"Yeah. Me too. What are you doing here?" I asked. *Keep him talking.* I picked up one of the chains that bound him to the others, running through loops in the prisoners' manacles.

"We got an anonymous tip that the Ellison Institute was going to be the site of the next set of murders."

I nodded encouragingly, trying to decide whether or not to attempt to break the chain. If I broke it, all these people would be free. They would still be wearing manacles, but at least they wouldn't be chained together. And while that might be a good thing in theory, I wasn't sure that thirty or forty loose mental patients would add much clarity to the situation on the ballroom floor.

And I wasn't entirely certain I wanted to know—or give away—how much strength my connection to Reese might give me.

*Oh, what the hell. How could it possibly get any worse than it already is?*

I took the chain between both hands, closed my eyes, and pulled with all my strength, feeling power dance along that invisible silver cord connecting me to Reese. There was a deep creaking noise, and then one of the links slowly pried apart.

"There," I said, pulling the other links off of it. "That'll give you motion, at least." I peered at the manacles. "I don't know if I can get those off without hurting you. Any idea who has the keys to these?"

I looked into Chandler's face and found that he was staring at me in sheer terror, his eyes huge. "Are you one of them?" he choked out.

Instead of answering, I leaned down to pull on the fabric and peek under the curtain. Iverson's men were pouring into the ballroom, covering one another as they took out vampire after vampire. The wooden dance floor was a slick mess of brains and blood. People screamed, guns popped, but the curtains muffled the noise.

"I'm with them," I said, motioning to Chandler to join me in looking out under the curtain. I pointed to a group of Iverson's men in the process of killing a vamp who had been draining one of their officers.

Chandler leaned back on his heels and nodded. Apparently, men in SWAT gear made him feel safe. I wasn't sure Chandler was feeling entirely himself, but at least he wasn't sobbing inconsolably like the woman next to him, or screaming that the world was ending.

I pulled my .45 out of its holster and handed it to him. "Take this," I said. He handled the weapon professionally, checking to make sure it was loaded, looking through the sights. Finally, he nodded. The gun seemed to give him a little of his confidence back.

"Get these people out of here," I said. "Don't shoot anyone until you see the fangs. The bullets are new—they'll take off a vamp's head."

Reese sidled around the edge of the curtain, and then came to stand beside me. "You okay?" he asked.

I saw Chandler's eyes widen as he caught a glimpse of fang.

"But not this one." I grabbed Chandler's gun hand and forced it down to keep him from aiming at Reese. "This one's with us."

"Okay," said Chandler, much more calmly than I might have in his situation. "Is there anything else I need to know? Any other friendly vampires I should avoid shooting?"

Reese shrugged.

"I don't think so," I said. "I don't know if there are any exits other than at the front, so I don't know how you're going to get these people out. That's going to have to be up to you. Dallas PD should have cleared the rest of the hotel by now. If you can get to an officer, or get out of the ballroom, they can help evacuate this group too."

Chandler nodded. "What about you?"

"We've got things to do," I said. "Ready?" I asked Reese.

"Ready as I'll ever be." He spoke in his usual drawl, but I felt excitement sparking along our bond, infusing me with his anticipation for the fight.

"Okay, then," I said. "Let's go."

Reese grinned at me and held up the curtain. "Ladies first."

"I'm pretty sure ladies don't carry as many weapons as I do," I said, grinning back at him.

As we ducked under the curtain, I heard Chandler popping out orders to the people with him. "Okay, everyone. Listen up! FBI here. I need your attention!"

Yeah, he was definitely doing better than I would have under those conditions.

As Reese and I stepped out to the edge of the stage and looked over the carnage below us, he reached over and took my hand and counted. "One, two, three."

We jumped, up and out, over the dais, and farther, almost to the middle of the ballroom.

For a moment, it felt like flying.

And then we landed and began fighting.

We moved in perfect harmony, twisting and turning, staking every vampire who dared come close to us. We were a perfectly balanced killing machine. It was like nothing I'd ever experienced before.

There were more of them than us, but all they had were their teeth and their super vamp strength.

Reese and I had more.

And we were winning—until our own dead began to rise and fight against us.

I don't know who was the first to notice it, but Tech One broadcast the info. "Watch out for vamps in SWAT gear! Our dead men are rising. Repeat: Our dead are rising as vampires."

I faltered, staggering out of step with Reese. He stumbled too, shaking his head and blinking.

A tall, thin female vampire came up from behind him, teeth bared. Without even looking at her, Reese slammed a stake back behind him. She crumpled to the ground without a sound.

"Glad you saw that," he said wryly.

I shook my head, trying to dislodge a sudden double vision, showing me both what I saw and what Reese saw.

And suddenly, what I saw scared the hell out of me.

"Crap. Check it out," I said, but Reese had already spun around.

Chandler and one of the officers were leading the mental patients along the edge of the room toward the exit. This would keep them out of the way of most of the vamps—the majority of whom were still in the middle of the ballroom.

But they were leading all those people straight to a SWAT team member. And I could tell, even if Chandler couldn't, that the officer was now a vampire.

Reese and I took off at a run, shoving both humans and vampires out of our way, but I knew we wouldn't make it in time, not to save everyone.

Inspiration hit me—and I didn't even have to say it aloud.

*Bats.*

The moment I thought it, Reese came to a dead stop, took a deep breath, and closed his eyes. I circled around him, watching for anyone who might try to attack.

This time, I was prepared for the rush of heat through my body, and I clasped the hand he reached out toward me, never dropping my wary stance.

Power surged between us, as all around me, fights were breaking out. But there were fewer and fewer of them. The floor was bloodstained and damp, and bodies—both human and vampire—littered the ballroom. Out of one nearby pile, I saw a SWAT officer rise and turn toward me, fangs bared. With my free hand, I fished the little derringer out of the purse I'd managed to keep tied to my other wrist and shot the new-formed vamp right between the eyes. It twitched once, then snarled again, so I took careful aim and fired again. This time, the top of its head came off in a confetti-shower of brains and blood. Both eyes continued staring at me, though. I had barely enough time to wonder if the top of the head was enough when the vampire took one weaving step forward and crumpled to the ground.

I looked at the ceiling. Reese's call was working. Tiny black forms flitted across the blue and gold of the mural and then swooped down to congregate around the vampire-officer's head. He tried to wave them away, but more and more of the bats came swooping in through the doorways, landing on him until he was covered—until he couldn't be seen for all the bats on him.

Chandler's group had stopped when the bats first started attacking. The FBI agent had even taken a couple of potshots at them. I hoped he had missed. Now all of the patients stood still and watched.

More bats circled in. Within seconds, the vampire toppled over, screaming. But the screaming soon stopped, and as the bats lifted away, I saw why. They had ripped his head off.

Chandler cautiously began leading his people across the room again.

"Detective Davis?" Tech One said in my ear. "Did you see what I saw?"

"Depends on what you saw." I worked to keep my voice steady.

"A bunch of bats take out a SWAT officer."

"That officer was a vamp."

There was a momentary silence, and then there was no more time for talk, as another vampire moved to attack us.

Once again, Reese and I moved in flawless accord. He spun behind the vamp and grabbed him by the arms, pulling them backward so that the vamp thrust his chest out at me as I shoved my stake into his heart.

It was beautiful, like a symphony of death, the most amazingly, exquisitely perfect thing I'd ever experienced.

And then the lights went out.

They were probably out for less than a minute, but it was long enough to bring that perfection I'd experienced crashing down around me. I felt my connection to Reese weaken a tiny bit.

I froze for an instant. And in that instant, I felt a cold, thin arm wrap itself around my neck from behind. Equally cold fingers wrapped themselves around the hand with my stake in it, holding it still in a grip like icy iron.

"He isn't really on your side, you know," a voice whispered in my ear, the sibilants harsh and breathy against my cheek.

"Somehow, Richards," I said in my normal voice, "I don't trust what you might have to say." I began working my free hand around to my waist, fumbling as I tried to extract the stakes that were hidden in the folds of my dress.

"You should believe me," she whispered. "Mendoza made Reese. Turned him for a purpose. Groomed him. Appointed him administrator."

"Mendoza didn't turn Reese."

"Are you sure?"

I wasn't, of course. Reese had told me the Sanguinary had arranged for him to be turned, but not which vampire had actually done it.

"So what?" I said, finally getting one of the stakes free and twisting it around in my hand. "Reese isn't responsible for what Mendoza did." As I was about to spin out from under her and stake her, though, she slid her arm from around my neck and grabbed my only free hand.

"Oh, but he is, you see." She used my arms to jerk me back against her body. "It's what he wanted. He used Mendoza to get power. Exactly like he's using you. He'll kill you in the end too." She paused, and then whispered into my ear, "Just like he killed me."

I froze, her words tumbling down into my stomach, along with my heart. Images clicked through my mind.

Richards, sitting on a bed in a patient's room the night of the raid on the clinic.

I hadn't seen her again that night.

Reese, disappearing at about the same time Richards had, showing up later at the cathedral crime scene.

Reese telling me had met with Mendoza to finalize his plans.

*I almost believe you.*

I couldn't say the words out loud—could only barely think them.

I leaned my upper body forward a little bit, and then rammed backward as hard as I could. We both went tumbling, rolling through the dark over blood and bodies. Richards lost her grip on me, and I came up onto my knees, stake held out in front of me.

I sat there for a moment, concentrating on shutting down the channel between me and Reese. I didn't know if it worked, but a brief moment of dizziness passed over me as the auxiliary power came on and the lights came up again.

I shook my head to clear it.

Richards was on her knees in front of me, rubbing the back of her hand across her own split lip. The blood leaking from it indicated that she had fed recently, and well.

I saw her before she saw me. I lunged toward her as she looked up. The stake slid in past her ribs, and she started laughing aloud.

"You know it's true," she said. "And killing me won't change it." Then the stake hit her heart. I felt a bolt of energy run through the wood and into my arm. Richards's laughter died along with her body.

I kneeled over her for a moment, almost wishing I hadn't killed her before I could ask more questions.

Was she telling the truth?

Just how big a risk had I taken by coming to this ball tonight?

I stared around the room, trying to find everyone. Not Reese—I knew without looking that he was behind me, killing another officer-turned-vampire.

Apparently I hadn't shut down the channel between us all that effectively.

Could he feel my shock, my horror at the knowledge he had turned Richards?

I wanted to find the rest of my team. The human members of my team. The people whose motives I at least knew, even if I didn't always entirely trust or understand them. Most of the vampires were dead; most of the humans were still alive. I finally spotted them. Chandler was herding the mental patients out some exit I hadn't even known existed. Jeanie and Andre were back-to-back on the dance floor. Andre reloaded his gun while Jeanie fired at a female vampire in a long white dress. The dress was streaked with blood—and then soaked with blood as the vamp's head exploded and dripped down her shoulders.

Through one of the now-open doors at the front of the room, I could see the squad doc in the ballroom foyer, tending to wounded humans—both those from our team and the ones who had been with the vampires.

The surviving bloodgivers looked shell-shocked, and I hoped they would eventually recover. But even more of the bloodgivers had died with their vampires, protecting them until the very end.

"Hey, Cami?" Iverson's quiet voice came from behind me. "You okay?"

I didn't turn around. "How much of that did you hear?"

"What Richards said? All of it."

"Could you keep that to yourself for a bit?" It was a lot to ask, I knew, but I needed to have the chance to question Reese myself.

"You think it's true?"

"I don't know. But until I do, I don't want anyone using it against us."

There was a long pause, and then he placed a hand gently on my shoulder. "You know I've got your back."

"But?" I hated the way my voice quivered as I asked. Finally, I gathered the courage to turn and face my teammate.

"No buts." He shook his head and smiled, his eyes kind and warm. "I've got your back. Even if I sometimes might not like it."

"Thanks." I nodded. Clamping down on my emotions, I headed over to Reese, who had finished off the last of a small group of vamps that had circled him while I was talking to Iverson.

"Nice work," I said.

"Thanks," he replied. "Would have been better with you here, though. What happened?"

I shook my head. "I don't know. The lights went out and some vamp bitch attacked me. Then I got a little woozy."

Reese nodded. "Me too. Right in the middle of these guys. Could have been bad if I hadn't already convinced them they ought to keep their distance." He grinned at me. My stomach flipped in response, and I felt the connection between us try to reassert itself.

"I'm going to go help deal with any stragglers," I said.

He nodded and moved away.

I heaved a sigh of relief. Eventually, I would have to deal with him.

But not yet.

I started systematically moving through the room, turning over corpses and staking any that still had heads. It was messy work, and the bottom of my gown was already soaked in blood. And by the time I'd made my way through most of the room, so was the top of my gown. I'd lost my purse sometime after I'd used the derringer, and I couldn't remember the last time I'd seen the wrap.

And then, back against a far wall, I found Savage and Bier, the SWAT officers I'd met at Westlake. Savage was lying on the floor, a stake sticking out of his heart. Bier had Savage's head cradled on his lap, and tears were dripping down his face. He looked up at me as I approached.

"He tried to bite me." A catch in his voice left long pauses between the words.

"I'm so sorry," I said.

"No," Bier said, stroking the hair on Savage's head, "I'm sorry." He whispered into the corpse's ear, "So sorry I didn't save you."

I backed away slowly, leaving Bier alone with his grief. I planned to make sure Bier came with us when we left, but until then, he could sit with his partner's dead body.

I moved back to Iverson, and we stared out across the blood and the bodies in companionable silence for a moment.

"Nice work," he said.

"Thanks. I like to think it's what I do best."

He chuckled and might have had something to say, if it weren't for the fact that Boyd dropped down on him at that moment.

I don't know where the vamp had been hiding, but he landed so hard that I actually heard one of Iverson's bones break. The crunch was accompanied by a startled yelp.

I didn't have long to think about it, though, because Boyd was apparently aiming for me. He lunged, and I danced backward to avoid his grasp. He was screaming and cursing so incoherently that it took me a couple of minutes of skipping out of his way to figure out what he was saying.

"You're mad because someone killed your human?" I jumped over a corpse on the floor, backing away from the screeching vampire. "You're the one who thinks vampires and humans shouldn't have relationships," I said. Shaking my head, I stepped forward and slammed the stake into his heart.

As I pulled back from Boyd, I heard several pops from Iverson's sharpshooters and saw a row of tiny red holes appear on Boyd's forehead. The vampire's head exploded not once, but three times. It sent showers of gore into the air and back down onto me.

I plodded back to the very front of the room. Iverson was being carried over to a stretcher by two non-vamp SWAT officers, and his face was white and strained. The squad doc motioned to them, calling out instructions.

Jeanie was sitting on the floor by the door, reloading magazines. "Hey, girlfriend," she said as I leaned on the wall beside her. "How'd it go?"

I glanced up and saw Reese in a similar pose to my own, leaning against a wall across the room, watching me with a slight smile on his face.

"Okay," I said to Jeanie.

"Only okay?"

"Yeah. But that's still better than I anticipated." I slid down the wall next to her.

"Isn't that the damn truth," she said, lifting one forearm to brush her hair out of her eyes. But she winced as she did, and I saw a bandage tugging at the underside of her arm—clearly slapped on quickly in the heat of the battle, not meant to last long or do much more than staunch the flow of blood.

I hadn't felt Reese move up behind me, but I knew as soon as he caught the scent of Jeanie's blood. Our connection slammed through me, leaving me doubled over as Reese's senses overwhelmed my own.

*I want to slide my teeth into her veins, feel the hot rush of blood fill my mouth.*

*I want to feel her last breath flutter across my cheek.*

*I want her to die in my arms.*

I wish I could say it was that thought that stopped me. But it wasn't. It was Reese, stepping in between us. He held out his hand and helped her up. At the same moment, an iron band of pure will slid down around me, into me, keeping me still, restraining me from moving any closer to Jeanie.

Reese's willpower.

Then Reese turned his back on Jeanie. "Go," he said to her over his shoulder.

Eyes wide as she stared at us, she dragged in a deep breath—I hadn't even realized she had been holding it—and then walked away without ever looking back.

The interaction had lasted only the barest instant. No one else in the room had noticed it.

"Get me out of here," I rasped, shaking in reaction.

Reese nodded, pulling me in close to him and scanning the room between us and the exit. On our way out, he snagged an abandoned tuxedo jacket and wrapped it around me.

It might not have made any real difference, but it felt like protection, as did his hands across the backs of my shoulders.

And for the first time ever, I realized, his palms felt warm.

We were almost all the way through the entry when I saw the small, crushed satin of my mask peeking out from behind the door.

"Wait," I said, ducking down to pluck it off the floor.

Reese waited barely long enough for me to grab the mask, and then tugged me out the doors and down the stairs. "Don't make eye contact with any officers. Concentrate on looking official."

I did my best—but probably luckily, all the officers on hand were busy taking statements from the relatively few human survivors.

And as far as I could tell, Reese was the only vampire to have survived the attack.

It didn't take us long to get to a back service elevator, and from there to the first floor.

"You have a car back here?" I asked.

Reese made a noncommittal noise that I took to mean *yes*—and that actually meant he had arranged for his truck to be waiting for us on the far side of a back entrance, away from any official vehicles. He bundled me inside. As he moved into the driver's seat, I tossed my ear bud out the window.

I didn't want the techs hearing any more of my conversations.

By then I was shivering.

"What now?" I asked as he pulled the pickup down a side street.

He glanced at me without answering, and we drove in the general direction of his art gallery.

"Why did you retrieve that?" he finally asked, gesturing toward the small mask in my hands.

"I don't know," I said quietly. After that, I stared out at the lights slipping along outside my window.

But I was lying. I knew exactly why I had insisted on stopping to grab it at that last moment.

I had to stop for it, had to have it, because it was symbol, no matter how small, of my last innocent moments.

The last night I truly believed I was one of the good guys.

# Chapter 26

Reese ushered me to his guest bathroom, handing me a stack of clean towels and clothes.

I stared at them blankly for a few moments—I guess it had never before occurred to me that a vampire might need something so prosaic as towels. Or women's clothing.

The thought flashed across my mind that the clothes might have belonged to Leila. A spark of jealousy threatened to ignite, but I pushed it away in favor of ignoring thought altogether. Or trying to, anyway. I couldn't help but wonder if he had kept the dead woman's clothes as mementos, or if he had been unable to bring himself to get rid of them. And in either case, what it might mean that he had given them to me to wear.

What did it mean to share a bond with a vampire?

In the shower, I studied the water running down my skin, tracing the blue lines of veins, thinking of the smell of Jeanie's blood, hot and enticing.

I didn't think of Reese turning Leah Richards.

Instead, I tried to think of what came next.

We had survived having slaughtered the Dallas vampire elite. We had helped wipe out every local vampire member of the Sanguinary. Along with more humans than I had been able to count.

And I was still alive.

A few hiccoughing sobs wracked my body. I tilted my head against the tile and waited for tears to come.

They didn't.

The water ran cold before I finally stepped out of the stall and dressed in the jeans and T-shirt Reese had left for me. I dragged a brush through my wet hair and spun it into a loose bun behind my head.

I could feel my body begin to shake, as if in reaction, but also as if it belonged to someone else.

*I don't have time for a breakdown.*

I dressed and made my way to find Reese, who was waiting in the main showroom, twirling an awl through his hands.

"Mendoza was planning more than just the stuff at the ball," he said.

I stared at him warily but didn't respond.

"The private Sanguinary induction was happening at the blood house. That's part of why he had the ball at the hotel, to keep other people away from it." He paused, his gaze searching mine. "You want to check it out with me?" he asked.

*I'm not about to let you go alone.*

Smile lines formed around his eyes, even though the expression didn't touch his mouth. "You don't have to trust me yet. It's okay."

I nodded. "If there's still work to be done, I'm ready to do it," I said.

When Reese turned away from me, I could feel the echo of our connection, drawing us together, orienting me to him like the needle on a compass to north. The pull to him was both stronger than it had been and more internal.

As we walked back to the truck, the connection between us was undeniable—despite what he'd said about not trusting him. I could feel emotions swirling between us, a mix of hope, fear, desire, and power.

It all added up to something a little bit like love. Reese pulled his truck back onto the street, his truck's headlights shining on the ground in front of him, and headed west.

"You think there's anyone still at the blood house we'll need to watch out for?" I asked.

"Maybe," he said. "But no one we can't take care of."

I glanced over at him briefly, then longer to watch the play of streetlights over his squared jaw.

"What?" he asked, his gaze flicking in my direction.

"How much of this did you have planned?" I asked. I didn't look away, didn't dare blink for fear I would miss something.

He shrugged. "Some."

"Only some?"

His silence threatened to draw out—but I was equally determined to wait for him to answer. When he finally spoke, I almost wished he hadn't.

"I was waiting for my chances. When they came, I took them. I didn't foresee all of them, but I'm damn glad I grabbed them when the moment came." His voice was husky, and I was reminded of my own tearless crying in the shower.

"I don't regret a single thing," he said, almost inaudibly.

# Chapter 27

The blood house was quieter than it had been on any of my earlier visits—but I was different too, so it almost sounded louder, even with only our footsteps echoing through the main room.

No one came out to meet us, but the door had been unlocked, so I assumed that we weren't alone.

But there was no breathing, and everything was almost entirely still.

"There, I think," I said quietly, pointing to the door behind the bar. Reese nodded and we swung out away from one another to circle the bar itself, as if we had been working rooms together all our lives.

I drew my gun and led with it. We rounded the edge of the bar to find nothing but an empty space. I slid around to the side, my back against the wall, briefly patting down the swaying curtain before sidling up to the door that led to the back.

I met Reese's eyes out of habit, but I could feel that he was ready to go through. We swung around and he kicked the door open. It crashed against the doorframe, and we followed it through.

Hard concrete floors. Boxes and boxes of booze. Stainless-steel shelves holding bottles.

And a trapdoor leading down into the floor.

"Seems like they could have at least covered it with a rug or something," I muttered. "I don't think they're even trying."

Reese shrugged. "I don't think they had to."

I moved back to the doorway and peered into the empty club. "So is this normal? If Mendoza's gone, everyone's gone?"

"I don't know," he said, lifting the padlock that held the trap door closed. He tugged at it experimentally, chewing on his lip absently. "I don't think the blood house has been empty since vampires showed up. Makes me think I'm right—there's something here he didn't want anyone else to see."

"It's creepy," I said, moving back over to join him.

"Stand back." He gave one sharp, hard tug on the padlock. The lock itself stayed closed, but the door around it splintered.

"That wasn't very sturdy." I stepped closer and bent down to peer at the wood.

"I don't think it was meant to be." Reese handed me the padlock. The side that had been facing up was bright stainless steel. But the other side was covered in tiny red symbols, all over.

"What does this mean?" I asked.

"No idea." He dropped down onto the stairs leading down to the basement. "But I'm about to go find out." Holding out one hand to me, he grinned—that same reckless, cowboy grin I'd seen on him before. "Want to come with me?"

*Oh, what the hell.*

"Sure," I said, and followed Reese down the darkened stairway. About two-thirds down the steps I realized that I was seeing things much more clearly than I had anticipated—even the darkest corners seemed slightly illuminated by a bluish glow.

A slight swishing noise came from down the hall that was at the end of the staircase. I moved off the last step and turned my back to the wall, holding my gun loosely, but ready.

There were doorways along the hall, but no light shone out from them, and there were no noises from within. I was torn between clearing the hall and following Reese, who moved with single-minded purpose toward the door at the end of the hallway—the one door that did have light and sound coming from behind it.

In the end, my police training kicked in and I did a quick check of each room as I moved past. I couldn't keep anyone from coming in behind us, but I could at least make sure we hadn't left anyone to attack us.

The rooms were small, cell-like, and empty.

At least one had rust-colored stains on the floor. I didn't need the lab to tell me it was blood.

My methodical sweep through the hallway didn't put me far behind Reese, who had opened the doorway at the end and stopped. I assumed he was waiting for me, though he didn't look back, instead staring intently at the scene in front of him. As I came up behind him, he moved slightly to the side, allowing me to see around him.

"What the hell is that?" I breathed.

A wooden frame stood in the center of the room, a naked woman dangling from the center crosspiece. Various straps held her up, some of them attached to her by hooks jabbed through the meatiest parts of her body. Her arms were stretched out to the sides, her palms nailed to the wood behind her. Dried blood flaked along her skin next to gouges in arcane designs, matching the ones carved into the stand that was holding the woman mostly upright.

The entire contraption sat atop a pentagram within a circle, carved into the concrete floor, then traced in blood.

"More blood magic," Reese said.

I moved to step into the room, but Reese held me back, gesturing at the floor in front of us.

"What is that?" I knelt down to look closer at the white line along the floor.

"Salt, I think," he said. "Try to pass through."

I followed his gesture and pushed my hand against the apparently open doorway, hitting what felt like marble, hard and cool to the touch, invisible to the eye. "Any ideas?" I asked.

Reese took a step back, drawing me with him. He rooted in his pocket and pulled out a penny. With an underhand toss, he threw it into the room.

The coin bounced across the threshold and rolled into the room, fetching up at the crucified woman's feet.

I gasped when she lifted her head and opened her mouth, her breath rasping in what I think would have been a moan, or maybe even a scream, if she'd been able to speak.

"Oh, holy hell," I whispered. "She's alive."

Reese nodded. "I don't know if we can get in."

"We need to call an ambulance," I said.

"No." He shook his head. "Not until we break their connection to the other world. We can't let anyone else see this, Cami." The way he said my name felt like a weight across my shoulders. He stared into my eyes, and I fought against the pull I could feel him exerting. "We have to destroy their access to the magic—and whatever is in this room is part of that." He stared in through the doorway, his voice dropping to a whisper. "Can't you feel it?"

As soon as he said the words, I felt the magic crash against whatever blocked the doorway, waves of it beating in time to my heart and my breath, pounding against the inside of my skull.

"She needs help," I said, determined not to drop the subject.

Reese glanced at me, and the pressure against the inside of my forehead lessened. "Let's at least get into the room first."

I looked at him, then at the salt on the floor. "So is that supposed to keep us out, or the"—I paused, gesturing at the invisible waves still thumping against the open doorway—"magic whatever in?"

He narrowed his eye at the salt line. "Mendoza was down here. I can smell him. This can't be designed to keep vampires out, not permanently, or Mendoza wouldn't have been able to get back in. I don't know about humans."

"Any idea what that stuff will do if we let it out?"

Reese shook his head. "Not a clue."

"Okay. Brace yourself." I knelt down and brushed my hand across the line, breaking it into individual crystals.

I expected the magical waves to wash over me, but instead, they retreated into the room.

Like my connection to Reese, they hovered just outside my ability to actually see them—almost a silvery blue shimmer, now swirling around the base of the apparatus holding the victim.

This time when I pushed my hand out, it moved easily through the doorway. I stood, brushing the salt off my hands. Reese followed me to the young woman, stepping carefully to avoid making contact with the waves. When I reached out to touch the woman gently, she began thrashing back and forth, and the angry-looking wounds around the hooks began to leak sullenly.

"It's okay," I repeated over and over. "We're here to help." I spoke softly as I moved around the stand, trying to determine if there was an easy way to take her down. After a long moment, she finally quieted. At first, I thought she had finally heard me, but then I realized she had simply passed out.

When she lost consciousness, the swirling magic stilled, and then seemed to drain away.

"We need to help her," I said to Reese, who was scanning the equipment surrounding the scaffolding.

"In a minute." His square-tipped fingers ran across the page of a book on a stand behind the woman. "I think I can almost see how this works."

"Now," I said. "She needs help now."

Silence. He continued to examine the book, the table, the device—everything but the barely living woman hanging from it.

*We're all monsters*, he had told me once.

At this moment, I believed him.

I pulled my phone out of my pocket to dial 911, but we were too deep underground. "I'll be back in a minute."

Reese didn't even respond.

I emerged from the stairwell into the storage room, and was staring down at my phone when something hit me from behind, hard. I tripped over my own feet and went sprawling. Someone landed on top of me, growling, "Die, bitch!" in a little-girl voice.

Dahlia.

With a jerk, I pushed myself sideways on the ground and rolled over, my feet drawn up to my stomach and ready to kick. But Dahlia had landed beside me. I pulled a stake from my ankle holster, rocked to my feet, and stood up. Without taking my eyes off the vampire, I moved sideways, trying to use my peripheral vision to find the phone she had knocked out of my hand.

"What are you doing here?" I asked—more to keep her occupied than from any real desire to know.

"You planned this," she snarled. "You killed them all. Everyone who mattered to me."

"You're a quick one." I took another step. Dahlia followed.

"How did you get out?" I asked. "Why didn't someone stake your screechy ass?"

With an inhuman shriek, she leaped toward me. I spun back out of her way, and she followed. We danced around the storeroom that way, Dahlia lunging and me ducking, shoving shelves, and throwing bottles at her while I waited for an opportunity to use my stake. I was half-waiting for Reese to show up and even the odds.

*Unless this is part of his plan.*

I stumbled as the thought hit me, barely catching myself in time to swing around behind a stack of boxes and avoid Dahlia's swipe at me.

Right now, Reese and I were the only ones who knew that the Sanguinary had a victim here.

We had killed all the local Sanguinary members.

If Dahlia killed me, Reese would be the only one who knew that the blood magic was pooling here.

And I didn't trust him enough for that to happen.

I moved along the wall, grabbing a bottle of whiskey on my way past a shelf, testing its weight in my hand, and eyeing the distance to my target. Her lips curled up in an ugly smile, and I saw her prepare to pounce.

Then my phone sang out, and I saw Dahlia hesitate—saw her gaze flicker toward the side of the room for the barest moment.

At least, that's what I thought at the time. Now I'm pretty sure it was a ruse, designed to draw me in. Because when I dove in to take advantage of her moment of inattention, she was waiting for me. My stake was centimeters from her chest when her hand, as cold and hard as ice, grasped my wrist, halting its progress and holding it still.

She used my forward momentum to spin me around and shove me against a wall. The whole thing felt like it moved in slow motion, but it took less than a heartbeat for her to pin me and bury her fangs in my neck.

I think I screamed.

This was nothing like Reese's blood-taking. There was no seduction, no gentle caress. It was hard and fast and brutal.

For an instant, I saw clearly past the veneer of civilization that the vampires wore, to the horror that had haunted humanity's nights for eons.

Fifty years until this monstrosity ruled.

*And I won't be here to stop it.*

The room wavered around me, the lights sputtering in and out. Or maybe, I realized, it was me—my consciousness flickering and fluttering. A bone-deep languor settled in my limbs, and I drooped in the vampire's arms. She followed me down to the ground, sucking in time to the frantic pace of my heart's pumping.

I closed my eyes as the chill from her hands spread throughout my entire body.

When her mouth ripped away from my neck, I could barely summon a whimper, even as my flesh pulled away with her teeth.

The room felt very far away, and a warmth drifted in from some other place, wrapping me in a soft blanket of silence. For an instant—or maybe eternity—I was done.

# Chapter 28

Noise penetrated my silent cocoon first. Someone calling my name.

*Reese.*

*He wants me to stay.*

And with the knowledge came awareness, and pain.

I was still in the storeroom—I wasn't sure how much time had passed. I opened my eyes, and the first thing I saw was Reese, staring intently into my face.

Where was Dahlia?

"That's it," Reese said. "Open your eyes. I need to know this is okay, Cami."

"Wha—" A half-gurgled noise, barely recognizable as speech, bubbled out of my throat. Almost frantic to warn him about the other vampire, I tried to lift my head, to look around the room, but that sense of an iron will holding me motionless returned.

"Hush." Reese's voice came to me, soothing and soft. "I staked her. Dahlia's gone." Reese closed his eyes briefly, and warmth flowed through the thread that connected us, swirling around and around until I could almost see it growing, a blue-white rope tying us together, heart to heart.

*Even if he is a monster?* I wondered.

*Even then,* some deeper part of me answered.

I wasn't sure if the answer was my own, or his.

"I don't have any other choice, Cami." He pulled my head onto his lap. "If I don't change you, you'll die. Please tell me *yes*." He held his wrist to his mouth, prepared to bite into it for me.

Change me?

My breath rattled in my chest, and as I looked into Reese's eyes, I knew it was true. If he didn't turn me soon, I wouldn't survive.

Could I manage that?

Could I become the very thing I hunted and still remain myself? Or would it be better to slip back into that warm silence and let others take over the fight?

*What others?*

Could I keep my allegiance to the human world, even if I let Reese turn me?

The bond between us flared to life as an image of former SWAT members rising as vampires in the Adolphus ballroom flashed across my mind.

"You'll still be yourself, Cami," Reese whispered. "Because you are part of me, I can make sure of it." I didn't know if I heard his sob, or simply felt it as if it were my own.

"I promise," he whispered.

Fifty years before everyone was either a vamp or vamp food.

I couldn't let that happen.

"Do it," I whispered, my voice barely displacing the air around us.

Reese stood and lifted me into his arms in one fluid motion. My head drooped back against his arm, despite my attempt to lift it.

"Hold on," he whispered to me.

The room around me narrowed until I saw only his face, its clean, strong angles set in serious lines. When he began to move, everything faded to black for a moment—or maybe a lifetime.

Reese stepped behind a curtain into one of the bleeding rooms and sat down, holding me gently in his lap.

I wanted to tell him that he didn't have to be so careful, because I couldn't feel anything. But I couldn't speak, so I watched him as I concentrated on the breath that rattled through my chest—pulling it in, and pushing it back out.

*Breath is life.*

But even as I thought it, I knew it was wrong.

Breath didn't matter.

Not anymore.

Reese turned and placed me on the cushion, sliding to his knees beside me even as I slipped out of his arms. Never breaking eye contact, he raised his wrist to his mouth and bit down, hard.

And then he was leaning over me, sliding his fangs into my neck, back into some of the several half-healed wounds from before. This time it hurt, and I tried to cry out, but all that emerged from my ravaged throat was a strangled whimper.

My heart stuttered in my chest, beating out a tattoo that slowed, and then sped up again for a moment as a last surge of adrenaline sped through my system. My vision blurred and went dark around the edges.

The next thing I knew was heat, sliding into my mouth and down my throat.

*Blood is life.*

In that moment, I knew it was true.

"Swallow," Reese ordered.

I tried to follow his command, choked, then tried again. Hot blood ran down my chin and onto my neck, mingling with the sticky mess already there. On the third attempt, I managed a convulsive gulp.

After that, I don't remember much but the warmth moving back through my body, circulating through my almost-dry veins. When Reese pulled his wrist away from my mouth, I whimpered and grabbed at his arm.

"Wait here," he said. "If we're going to get out of here, you have to feed."

I shook my head, pulled at his hands as he stood up. "I can't," I said. "I can't feed on a human."

He stared down at me for a long moment as if deciding whether or not to tell me the truth. When he finally spoke, his voice was low. "You have to. You won't be yourself much longer if you don't feed."

The image again flashed through my mind of the SWAT officers in the ballroom—I'd do anything not to become what they had become.

"Cami, you have no choice. I can't keep you here, like this, much longer." The connection between us pulsed hot, this time burning through my veins as well as against my skin, and I realized Reese had activated it on purpose.

He spoke more urgently as I still hesitated. "This is what you agreed to. I'll be here, and I'll make sure you don't kill her. But if we're going to win this war, then you are going to have to accept the things you have to do, just as I did. Starting now."

He didn't wait for a response before once again picking me up, then spinning on his boot heel and sliding out from behind the curtain. I wrapped my arms around his neck and buried my face in his neck.

As he carried me through the storeroom, past Dahlia's lifeless, crumpled body, and down the stairs, I thought about what he had said.

He was right, of course. I would do whatever I had to do to save this world.

*But I don't have to like it.*

# Chapter 29

Downstairs, Reese gently placed me on the floor so I could lean against the wall.

He lifted the woman from the wooden stand by breaking off the hooks at the point where they connected to the stand, leaving them in place through her skin. She screamed at the first one and a blue light flared from the carvings in her skin for an instant.

I could feel the magic again, beginning to swirl around me.

And every time she screamed, the invisible waves crested.

The shrill of her voice was overpowered by the rocking of the waves and beating sound of the hot silk running through her veins. I leaned toward her as she turned to look at me, and I knew the moment she saw the hunger in my eyes.

I stared into her eyes. I wanted a tear to fall from those lashes—wanted to lick it away while more piled behind her frightened gaze, as she shivered, frozen and still and afraid.

I could smell her fear.

I wanted to taste it.

My jaws ached.

Prey.

Then she passed out.

My lust faded to hunger. I was glad of it.

Reese placed her gently on the floor and beckoned to me to join him from where I stood, leaning heavily against the table holding the bookstand and various other arcane instruments.

"We have to hurry," he said. "I've called 911. The ambulance will be here soon."

More than that, some part of me knew that if I didn't feed soon, the transformation wouldn't take.

*I won't survive for very long.*

It was true, but some other part of me knew it for the rationalization it was.

I didn't want to die.

My jaw ached for a moment, and I felt fangs slide into place. I knelt down, and glanced at Reese. He pointed at a spot on the woman's neck.

But I didn't need the guidance.

I could hear her heart beating, the swish of the blood as it moved through her veins. I could see the slight pulse of blue under her skin. And I could smell the blood, calling to me.

I inhaled deeply against her neck, and then pushed my fangs through the skin.

She gasped and jerked, and her heart fluttered, the vein pulsing in time to the rapid beat.

The blood that filled my mouth was as hot as Reese's had been, but different—softer, silky and smooth.

It filled me with a strength that Reese's blood hadn't.

And with it came the swirling waves of magic, rolling in and through me. Reese gasped as warmth flooded me like the pulsing of the sun. With it came life.

Never-ending.

I lost myself, and I don't know if I would have pulled back, had Reese not taken me by the shoulders and tugged me away. "That's enough," he said.

I licked my lips, and then nodded.

I could hear the faint wail of ambulances, the sound of people moving around upstairs as the paramedics crashed in through the front door.

The few remaining magical waves—those that I hadn't absorbed as I fed—had receded. But I could see them now, glowing with a deep blue light that called out to me.

It matched the glowing cord that connected me to Reese.

And it was nothing that belonged in this world.

"Ready?" Reese asked me.

I didn't ask what he meant.

I didn't have to.

I simply nodded, and he took my hand.

"Let's go, then" he said, pulling me back to the book on the table. Reese flipped it open, and then ran his finger across the lines on a page. I couldn't read them, but in a quiet voice, he spoke the same words Mendoza had said in the ballroom.

The waves coalesced into a blue light that flashed in front of the crucifixion stand, and the woman on the floor let out a long, sorrowful wail.

The light grew in proportion to her scream. A hot, breathless wind whipped through the room—a wind that, I realized, was coming through the light.

"Where does that lead?" I yelled over the air blasting through the room.

Reese didn't respond, staring wide-eyed as the blue light grew to the size of a door and began to bulge toward us. The symbols on the stand glowed the same color, as did the wounds on the woman's skin, all three beams of light meeting in the middle of the room, widening to become an oval taller than Reese.

"Destroy the book." Reese pulled a cigarette lighter from his pocket and tossed it to me. "It will take blood, I think. But wait until I'm back." I caught the lighter and spun around to the book on the stand. The pages were glowing the same shade of blue as the light, the symbols in the book shooting light straight to the ceiling.

I could feel the same glow within me.

I didn't know if my blood would do, but I certainly wasn't going to take any more of the poor woman's if I could help it. We had done enough to her.

In any case, Reese had her in his arms and was striding toward the doorway and the stairs.

Moments later, he was back by my side. "The paramedics have her," he said. "Let's do this."

I concentrated until my jaw ached again, and then I slid my fangs into my own wrist. I held it over the book, dripping blood over the symbols, and then smudging the dark red stains to occlude the glow of the arcane markings. When the light had dimmed a bit, I held the cigarette lighter to one edge of the pages, waiting until they were curling and smoking before moving it to the other three corners in turn.

The wind in the room whipped hotter, and I could hear a scream inside it. Only when the top page was almost entirely blackened and the other pages glowing with red embers did I look back at the doorway-shaped blue light.

And for an instant, I saw a snarling, fanged face pushing through the door, framed by hands curved into claws.

We made eye contact, and my breath caught in my throat—that life-breath I was no longer supposed to have, holding in a way that wasn't supposed to affect me any longer. The blue of the light swept out from the face's eyes and into mine, power pulsing down through me, touching the part of me that connected to Reese, leaving me dizzy with the strength of it.

The bulge receded. Reese moved to the doorway as the book toppled off its stand and onto a nearby table, where flames leapt up among the papers surrounding it.

Reese stared at the growing fire for a moment and said, "Let it burn." Then he held out his hand to me.

"We won't be able to come back this way," I said.

He nodded, holding my gaze with his own. "We don't belong here, anyway. Not any longer."

He took a step back so that his heel barely brushed the blue light. He lifted his other hand toward me, both palms turned up, and smiled. "We can do this, Cami," he said. "We can fix it so the monsters don't win—can't even get through. But I think maybe we have to do it from the other side."

I didn't know if I had chosen the right side, or if Reese could be trusted.

But I knew he was right.

I didn't belong here now.

*We're all monsters.*

And this might be the only possible chance to keep the world from going under the darkness.

Fifty years before the vampires won.

But maybe I could stop them.

As black smoke filled the room and the flames swirled in the wind from the magical passage between worlds, I reached out to take Reese's hands.

We stepped through together.

# Epilogue

Moonlight glinted off of the high-desert dunes in the distance. I slung my knapsack over my shoulder and followed Reese out into the tavern's courtyard. "Are you sure the bartender knows what he's talking about?"

"He's too afraid of vampires to lie to me." Reese grimaced, speaking over his shoulder as he walked into the stable. "Humans are definitely in the minority here. He would never consider lying. It would be too dangerous."

I waited, tapping my foot impatiently while Reese saddled the two animals he'd managed to trade for on our third night here. Like everything else in this dimension, the creatures were slightly different from their Earth counterparts—their hooves, for example, were split, more like antelopes' than horses' feet. I called them the "not-horses."

In a fit of whimsy, Reese had given them spectacularly ill-fitting names: Sunshine and Sugar Pie.

"Sunshine bites," he warned me the first night we rode.

I had the bruises to prove it.

I mounted the cantankerous Sunshine and wheeled her around to follow Sugar Pie's clattering steps out onto the cobblestone streets.

It had seemed like a simple task, back at home: go through the portal, find out what the Sanguinary was hiding about the other side, and shut down the entry into our world from this one.

I don't know what I had expected, but it wasn't an entire planet, complete with people, families, children. Stars in the night sky that didn't match the ones I knew. A whole other universe. And somewhere over here, someone who was taking advantage of the holes the Sanguinary had been ripping open between worlds.

Whatever had been trying to push through when Reese and I had come across hadn't been waiting for us. We didn't know if it had passed over to our world, or if it left when it saw us coming.

Without us to hold it open, the portal had collapsed in on itself, taking its magic with it, leaving us standing alone in a quiet, cobblestoned alley.

But we had discovered other magics in this world—either that, or we'd honed the magic of our connection. Every time we touched, it sparked between us, the heat growing stronger, more palpable.

And the more we touched, the more we wanted to.

Even now, I could feel the strands of power stretching between us, tying us to one another. If I squinted, I could almost see them. Neon bands, blue and yellow and green, binding us with that mix of hope, fear, desire.

Maybe even love.

At the edge of the small city, a gated wall separated the street from the town, though keeping the streets free of sand was a losing battle.

No one guarded the gate. Humans here didn't go out after dark.

The road widened outside the wall, and Reese reined back to ride beside me. "This caravan is setting up to do some trading tomorrow. According to the bartender, they don't come into cities, and from what I could tell, the reason they stay outside the walls has something to do with their magic-users and portals."

"From what you could tell?"

He shrugged. "It's a miracle we can talk to these people at all."

"Or some kind of portal magic." That was my answer to just about everything these days.

Reese's sound of agreement was almost swallowed up in the jingle of the not-horses' harnesses.

The caravan's campsite was almost an hour's ride away. The glow of lights had been growing steadily for at least twenty minutes, so we weren't surprised when we crested a hill and saw the brightly colored silk tents clustered below us.

But the sight of an enormous blue portal pulsating from the center of the camp took my breath away.

Reese let out a low whistle and his drawl came out in full force. "I think maybe we should scope these folks out before we try talking to them."

"Unless they have a guard out." I glanced around me, peering into the darkness, wishing that the portal glow hadn't ruined my night vision.

"I don't think so." Reese settled his hat on his head and turned Sugar Pie back down the hill. "If they're anything like the vamps in town, they're too sure of themselves. No one here would cross them, so there's no need to post a guard."

We tethered the animals behind a small dune, but in sight of the road. If something happened to us, someone would take them. We weren't quite willing to send them back toward town without more information about what we might find in the camp.

"How much power does a portal that size take?" I murmured as we made our way slowly around the perimeter of the grounds.

"I think maybe that's what happens with thirteen sacrifices," Reese whispered.

I sent up a small prayer that we really had stopped the Sanguinary. What had happened back on Earth after we left?

If we closed down the portals on this side, would we be stuck here forever?

*It doesn't matter*, I told myself for the umpteenth time. *As long as we keep the vampires from taking over.*

Even if I was one of *them* now.

On the far side of the encampment, we found a small rise in the ground, just enough to hide us in the shadows as we stretched out prone behind it, peering over and down into the center of the circle of silk tents where the blue light of the portal flickered.

In front of the opening stood a tall, muscular man, dark-skinned and bald, wearing only a loincloth, his hand resting in a gesture of benediction on the man kneeling before him. He sang out incomprehensible words, his voice keening into the night and stretching out to the portal in long, thin strands of bright power.

The portal echoed the tones back to him, amplified and heightened, the sound pulling power from the ground as it pulsated across the desert sand.

The power surrounding the priest sparkled and expanded, brushing against the circle of figures sitting around the pair in the center.

Reese reached down and grabbed my hand. Our own energy sparked back and forth between us, encircling us.

Protecting us.

As the priest finished his song, he raised both arms and pulled all of the resultant power into himself until he glowed as brightly as the portal and the young man's worshipful expression was spotlighted by the shine.

The priest dropped his palm back onto the supplicant's head, light pouring from his hand. And the man, already on his knees, screamed and dropped to all fours. The priest stepped back as the figure in front of him began writhing, the sound of screaming enveloped in a rising hum that exploded in a flash of power washing over all the tents.

I grasped Reese's hand even harder. The splash of power sparked against our own protective barrier, but didn't breach it.

When the dazzle faded from my eyes, I barely contained my gasp.

Where the young man had knelt now stood a wolf-like creature.

Over the next few minutes, as the priest alternately raised and lowered his hand, as if conducting a symphony, the adolescent changed forms, back and forth—human to animal, and back again.

At some unspoken signal, or perhaps when he was satisfied by the quality of the shifts, the priest nodded, and the boy stepped through the portal. Within moments, the opening shrank away, closing with little fanfare.

Everyone stayed where they were for a few moments longer, giving their eyes time to adjust to the gentle starlight. With a few murmurs, the crowd began to stir.

In silent accord, Reese and I slid down the rise and made our way back to our mounts.

We had been on the road, headed to town for at least fifteen minutes before either of us spoke.

Reese broke the silence. "That was a werewolf, wasn't it? A fucking *werewolf*."

I nodded. "And I think they were sending it back to Earth."

We stared at each other in dismay, our emotions roiling back and forth along the connection between us.

Finally, I said aloud what we both already knew. "We can't do this by ourselves."

Reese reined Sugar Pie closer and reached across the distance between us to clasp my hand. "Then we'll find the help we need. Together."

# ABOUT THE AUTHOR

Margo Bond Collins writes urban fantasy, contemporary romance, and paranormal mysteries. She lives in Texas with her daughter and several spoiled pets. Although writing fiction is her first love, she also teaches college-level English courses online. She enjoys reading romance and paranormal fiction of any genre and spends most of her free time daydreaming about heroes, monsters, cowboys, and villains, and the strong women who love them—and sometimes fight them.

Did you enjoy this book? Drop us a line and say so! We love to hear from readers, and so do our authors. To connect, visit www.boroughspublishinggroup.com online, send comments directly to info@boroughspublishinggroup.com, or friend us on Facebook and Twitter. And be sure to check back regularly for contests and new releases in your favorite subgenres of romance!

Are you an aspiring writer? Check out www.boroughspublishinggroup.com/submit and see if we can help you make your dreams come true.